W153s

The
Scathach and
Maeve's Daughters

Books by Mary Alexander Walker

Brad's Box
The Scathach and Maeve's Daughters

The Scathach and Maeve's Daughters

by Mary Alexander Walker

Atheneum   1990   New York

Collier Macmillan Canada
Toronto

Maxwell Macmillan International Publishing Group
New York   Oxford   Singapore   Sydney

Atheneum
Macmillan Publishing Company
866 Third Avenue
New York, NY 10022

Collier Macmillan Canada, Inc.
1200 Eglinton Avenue East
Suite 200
Don Mills, Ontario M3C 3N1

First edition
Printed in the United States of America
Designed by Nancy B. Williams
1   2   3   4   5   6   7   8   9   10

Library of Congress Cataloging-in-Publiation Data

Walker, Mary Alexander.
The Scathach and Maeve's daughters / Mary Alexander Walker.— 1st
ed.
        p.   cm.
Summary: In the eighth century, Scathach, the ancient shape-
shifting female champion, appears to Maeve Moira, the daughter of a
Celtic High King, and, pleased with her character, promises that her
daughters—and the daughters of their daughters—will survive and
possess Maeve's qualities.
ISBN 0–689–31638–0
[1. Celts—Fiction. 2. Space and time—Fiction. 3. Supernatural—
Fiction.] I. Title.
PZ.W15362Sc   1990
[Fic]—dc20   90-141
                                                                  CIP
                                                                   AC

TO SPENCER, JESSICA, NANCY, AND IN MEMORY, TIM

Scathach, "the shadowy one of a thousand faces" lived on an island near Scotland and was the greatest magical female champion of her time. Heroes from all the Celtic nations would travel to study with her for she alone knew the magic which made them inconquerable. Her most famous student was the great Irish hero of legend, Cuchulain.

De Jubainville,
The Irish Mythological Circle
and Celtic Mythology

... Cuchulain studied ... with Scathach until he had learned all the magical arts ... and all the feats of a champion. ... And Scathach told him what would happen in the time to come, for she had the Druid gift.

The Book of Leinster,
colophon to Tain Bo Cuilnge
(twelfth-century manuscript)

CONTENTS

1.

Maeve Moira – Eighth Century

> Clotho, the youngest of the three Fates,
> weaves the fabric of lives. Mostly, she uses
> coarse ordinary thread, sometimes silk, and rarely
> a fine skein of gold.
>
> Myth

Wherein Scathach, the ancient female champion, appears as an old woman to Maeve Moira, the daughter of a Celtic High King. Scathach explores the young woman's character with her magic, and pleased with what she finds, promises that Maeve's daughters—and the daughters of their daughters—will survive and possess Maeve's qualities.

In the last rays of sunset, Maeve Moira was tired from walking all day and from the heavy clothes she wore. Though her years were only sixteen, she carried herself like the royalty she was, the daughter of a High King of Ireland.

White woolen the cloak covering a silvery fur long vest, silver the scrollwork medallion clasped at her throat. Green the silk dress touching the tops of her doeskin shoes. She usually rode in her own white chariot flanked by four other chariots of sky blue and silver. Now her legs ached and her shoes were scuffed and dusty from this unaccustomed journey, searching for her pet bull calf.

When the baying of the hounds woke her that morning, she saw from her window, not only the first hazy light, but her little brown bull scampering wildly toward the oak woods. She quickly dressed for the frosty morning and followed him, rashly, alone.

Deep red the bracken she tramped through, past the green-barked yew, edging around a herd of wild swine, then grazing deer, and a badger's brood; finally the green masses became sandy, rocky wilderness.

She passed the blackened stones of houses burned by raiding Vikings. Storehouses of seed for planting had been looted and razed. They were only hummocks now with weeds and gorse springing around. So little was left after the Viking plunder, a whole new Teltown had to be built.

She hurried beyond the great Pictish stone, fifteen feet high, covered with carved design and unreadable language. She shivered at the cry of the wind that whirled past the monument towering so high it cast a long, black shadow across her path.

She frowned. When night fell, she could not track Little Brown's footprints. She would never find the little dim-witted bull in the dark—and he must be dim-witted to run away from his mistress—and into a terrain she did not know: unfamiliar cliffs, buttes, great stones. It seemed a noinen since she had left the glens of home; could it be only since dawn that she had followed the prints of the straying bullock?

4

She watched the fog already drifting like gray smoke over the mounding rocks in front of her and she drew her cloak more tightly about her, pulled the hood closer over her red hair, and puzzled over Little Brown's tracks. Why had the bull's tracks looked so strange? As if he stopped, stomped, then madly surged again in wild running as if chased by something. But how could he be pursued? There were no other footprints, no other tracks.

Maeve did not know that it was *she* who was being pursued; Little Brown had not been chased—he had been driven, but by feet that made no tracks.

Intent on discerning the footprints, Maeve Moira did not see the shadowy figure always to her left, sometimes behind a cairn, sometimes hobbling over a mound, sometimes peeping from behind a blackthorn or a whortlebush. When Maeve stopped to ponder where to make her fire for the night, her shadowy pursuer shuddered as the mists swirled in the crannog where she lurked.

It was the Scathach, the female champion of renown, a trainer of the most famous warriors in the ancient isles, possessor of strange powers; she was as old as the mists that drifted around her shoulders, and, perhaps, as old as the moon.

The Scathach knew where Little Brown was. She had driven him over a bank of rocks and he was caught there now, his foot locked between two stones where he had clambered in his headlong running. He thought he was abandoned and lost forever. His despair was so great that he did not even cry out.

The Scathach had plans for Little Brown and now she did not hesitate to carry them out: Suddenly the little bull felt a scorpion sting on the flank and he instinctively let out a calf's bawl for his mother.

Maeve, at the sound of that familiar bawl, began springing agilely over the terrain as if her feet had wings.

"Little Brown! Little Brown! Stay! Stay!" she called. As Maeve reached the top butte, she could see him, and just as suddenly—another sting in the rear—he jerked his foot from between the stones, tearing hide and flesh, blood spurting, and he galloped bawling, stumbling to his knees, scrambling up, and dashing toward the stream at the bottom of the bank.

"No, no!" Maeve screamed, running after him. But too late to stop his headfirst plunge into the stream—splashing, bawling, gurgling. Maeve lunged forward and grabbed his flailing tail as his head disappeared under the water. Heavy as he was, she teetered on the bank for a moment, clutching the wild tail with all her strength. His head came up, eyes wild and terrified. He sank under the water, Maeve still grasping his tail.

"Little Brown," she yelled, and she began to inch her way backward, twisting her body and rolling until she could get a firm kneehold on a buried stone. She slowly swung him close to her face. In a last instant of consciousness, he smelled her, he saw her, and with the scantling of spirit left, his hind hooves caught in the riprap firmly and he heaved himself up in a lunge. He and Maeve were lumped in a sodden heap on the bank.

The Scathach nodded approval. The Scathach, chewing a blackthorn leaf she had picked in the glade, had watched the rescue from a snug cranny in the top of the rocks. Now she stroked her bristly chin and chuckled as Little Brown lay lifeless-looking on the earth. Maeve ripped a strip of cloth from the skirt of her dress and bound it around the bull's torn fetlock. Then she wrapped him in her long cloak, pillowing part of it under his head, consoling and comforting him in a whispered voice all the while.

Maeve scrabbled in her small leather pouch and, finding her flints, tried to fire little bits of twigs and dry grass she had raked together quickly with her fingers.

The Scathach tossed the leaf away, climbed out of the cranny, and crouching, crept silently among the boulders; she listened to the clicking of Maeve's flints as she tried to light a fire and heard her talking to Little Brown. Creeping along the bank of the dark torrent, the Scathach moved behind Maeve and slid over the bank and into the water.

Completely submerged, she raised one gnarled old hand above the surface of the murky water for Maeve to see. But Maeve's attention was on the fire-making and the little bull; she did not see the hand, and the clicking of the flints continued.

Now the Scathach made her hand transparent, the lumpy bones chalky under a layer of fleshlike clear jelly. When Maeve did not notice, she made her hand phosphorescent: a pale green glowing specter reflecting on the black surface.

But Maeve was desperately engrossed in making the fire, and murmuring encouragement to the silent bullock, she still did not notice the ghastly, ghostly hand sticking out of the water.

When the Scathach had gone by Maeve completely—unseen—she cursed, burbling under the water and started over again. This time, when in the most observable place, her hand suspended over the water—though she took care to be very near the bank—she drew all the oxygen out of her body and let go with a huge burp. When it bubbled to the surface it broke with an audible *glurk* and Maeve looked up. Her eyes widened in horror at the hand reaching out of the water, and the Scathach made her hand writhe beseechingly for help.

Maeve leaped forward and grasped the hand, pulled with all her strength—and the old woman, gasping, sodden, clinging to Maeve in pretended terror, climbed up the bank.

With her arm around her small shoulders, Maeve guided her away from the bank, anxiously asking, "Little Mother, Little Mother, what happened? Is all well with you?"

"Aye," snapped the old woman, "but cold. Take that cloak from around that churlish bullock and dry me."

"Nay, he is cold and injured, and I fear—I fear he is—" Maeve swallowed and started again, "I fear he is dying." Maeve whipped her arms out of her long fur vest. "But here, my vest will warm you, Little Mother—" Maeve stooped again to the twigs and flints. "If I can just light a fire, it will keep us all alive through the night," and she struck the flints.

Poof! The twigs exploded into a crimson blaze so suddenly that Maeve fell backward, staring in wonder at the roaring fire.

The old woman cackled, rollicking about it. "Aye, you want a fire!"

Maeve leaned over the little bull, snuggled the cloak closer to his body, and said, "Look, Little Brown, a wonderful fire—such a blaze—you will be warm." But Little Brown's eyes were closed, his body limp. Maeve sighed and reached for the piggin swinging on a braided thong from her filigreed silver belt.

"I have some cheese, Little Mother. Would you like some?"

The small figure huddled by the fire did not answer. Maeve held out the cheese to her. The sinewy hand grabbed it and shoved it into her mouth at once, smacking and chomping. Crumbs protruded and clung to her scraggly chin. Maeve handed her a heavy lace kerchief to use as a napkin as the crumbs fell on the fur mantle and down the ragged dress. The Scathach whisked the crumbs away and tied the kerchief around her gray, grizzled hair.

Again Maeve sat beside Little Brown. She placed her hand on his chest. Then she said, "He hardly breathes. His life goes."

The Scathach laughed loudly ... more a repeated snort than a human laugh.

With anger, Maeve looked at her. She said, "Why do you laugh when he dies?" Then her anger passed and she said sadly, "He is a dim-witted baby bull, it's true, because he ran away—but dear he is to me, Little Mother."

Quietly, they sat by the flickering fire; it cast rosy gleams on their faces, and turned the hollows of eye sockets and cheeks crimson. Around her face Maeve's hair glowed— threads of gold, red, amber—as if multicolored jewels had been sprinkled on her forehead.

The Scathach spoke, startling Maeve out of her reverie.

"Young One, what would you have?"

Maeve did not understand. "What would I have?"

"Yes, yes." The Scathach was impatient. "What would you have? What would you wish for?"

Maeve stroked the fur on Little Brown's sleek head, then sat deep in thought. Finally, she said, "I would have a kind heart and healing hands."

"Bah," said the Scathach, disappointed. "You have that already."

"No," answered Maeve. "All night I have sat with Little Brown, keeping him warm, stroking his head, calling his spirit back to me—he stirs not—"

"Aye, but on the morrow he will. He is but resting, gathering his strength," the old woman said.

Maeve put her hand on his chest again and her face brightened. "True, his heart beats like heavy rain." A slow smile grew on her face. "Then, I have healing hands?"

"Yes, yes," grumbled the old woman. "What would you have?"

"Then—then—" Maeve waved her hands in excitement. "Then I would have courage and wits—yes, Little Mother, that is what I would have—courage and wits!"

The Scathach glared at Maeve, at the scarlet hair framing her young face, her hands gold from the fire, the amber eyes sparkling with excitement; she saw her again tracking the bullock, straining to pull him out of the water, then having the grace to reach for the gnarled hand rising ghostlike out of the stream—"Oh, how little you know yourself, Young One. You ask for what you already have."

Maeve, scratching Little Brown softly between the ears, watched the old woman with astonishment.

"But," the Scathach continued, "I will give these to your

daughter and her daughter and to her daughter's daughters—your qualities shall be handed down through your blood through all the ages, and it shall be as I have said, and I shall ever watch to see that this is so, for I am the Scathach—"

The old woman tossed a handful of shale on the fire and it blazed sapphire and amethyst, and before Maeve could even blink, the old woman said, "Sleep now and you will forget what I have said and that I ever was—"

Without a word, Maeve, clad only in her silk dress, snuggled close to Little Brown and, on the cold earth, slept.

The Scathach curled into a round ball for a nap herself; in the long fur mantle, she was as round as a rolled-up cat with ears of lace sticking out—Maeve's kerchief. Before the mists and fog had time to seep into her old bones, she sat up; she did not need much sleep. Hungry again, she crept to the sleeping figure of Maeve; she searched in the piggin for cheese. Maeve stirred and rolled in her sleep.

"Quiet, Young One, quiet," the old woman murmured and Maeve was immediately stilled. But there were only the tiniest crumbs of cheese left in the piggin, which the Scathach drew out on the ends of her fingers, then licked them, her long pink tongue savoring each fragment. Then she wiped her hands in the soft fur of the mantle.

"I must look grand in this fur," she mused and she walked, daintily, skirting the rocks, to the water's edge.

The fog was dense there, a white mask over the water and clouds had covered the moon. Impatiently, the Scathach swung her right arm at the sky, then pointed a crooked finger at the clouds. They scudded across the sky as if a sudden wind had whisked them away; the moon's face, like a great pearl, appeared in the midnight blue.

With her left arm, she made three circles over the mist drifting on the water. Just as quickly, the mist parted in the middle and scurried to the right and the left, leaving a bright clear space before her where the moonlight shimmered on the still water. She leaned, then knelt; reflected in the mirrorlike surface was the Scathach's wrinkled face, her short square nose like a dollop of clay on her small flat face—but dangling over her forehead shone the white lace of the kerchief and around her shoulders reflected the silver hairs of the fur. She preened and chuckled at the sight of herself. She pulled the fur close around her scrawny neck, straightened the lace on her forehead and cackled aloud. Then quickly, she scrambled back to her feet, waved a hand at the heavens—clouds obscured the moon, and at the stream, mists hurriedly swathed it again. She stalked back to the fire muttering, "Old fool."

Clambering up on a high rock so that she could look down on the sleeping Maeve and the calf, she squirmed to make her bony rump comfortable. Then her squinchy eyes grew larger and bulged out with dark green fire gleaming and sparkling.

"Lo, let me see your spirit, Young One. Show me!" she commanded. Her hand grazed the rock where she sat and pieces came from it, like dust—she threw it on the fire.

Maeve disappeared. Though her green silk dress lay in disarray where she had slept, her body became invisible. In her place quivered a doe, sleek of coat, head held high, ready to leap, the great brown eyes tinted ruby in the firelight—

12

"Good, good. Soft and tender, but quick, quick—swift of foot," the Scathach muttered.

At the sound of the voice, the doe sprang, but the Scathach snapped, "Enough!"

Then she threw rock dust on the fire and the deer vanished. In her place was a shaggy she-wolf, with powerful shoulders and strong shanks, snuffling cautiously the scent of the woman and the smoke that drifted by her proud, furry nose.

"Ah, the leader, the caretaker of the clan. The faithful and the loyal." As the she-wolf turned her intelligent eyes to investigate the sleeping bull, the Scathach threw her hands in the air, the wolf vanished and Maeve was again asleep in her place by the fire.

The Scathach's head bobbed up and down in satisfaction. Her eyes became what they were at first, little brown pebbles. She rubbed her rough hands together contentedly. "Swift-footed as the deer and loyal and faithful as the she-wolf. Good. Good." Her leatherlike cheeks wrinkled in a smile. Then as the hour passed the mid of night, the mists rose higher and the chill became bitter. She made the fire leap and she hunched her skinny shoulders against the cold. She fell into deep thought, her chin resting on her chest as if in sleep. At last she began to frown. She shook herself out of her stupor and focused her eyes on Maeve. Again, they became green fire, standing out from her face like balls of emerald, shooting sparks.

"The skin of the deer is a shoe for the feet and for vestments. And what of the wolf skins covering floors of the dwellings of men? They clean their muddy feet on those wolf skins and dogs drool on their bones there. No, it is not enough, Young One, to be gentle and clever and quick as the deer. It is not enough to be loyal and wise and faithful as the powerful she-wolf." The green eyes glinted and gleamed and glittered. "Have you nothing more? More than a skin to cover the foot or the floor? Have you not more spirit than that? Show me, Young One, show me!" and she hurled rock dust into the fire.

Whoof! Such an enormous creature leaped from the fire and billowed into the heavens, towering, that the Scathach fell backward, rolled over a rock, and crouched behind it to view what had appeared.

Shining gold and bronze scales loomed far over her head; claws dangled from glistening, scaly limbs; higher still the Scathach looked and saw the elegant head, nostrils breathing bright ribbons of flame.

"Dragon!" the Scathach whooped.

Fiery eyes loomed in the blackness, casting light before them like moons. The great wings flapped. Fire scattered and dust and rocks and shale whirled in the air. The Scathach coughed, and the gigantic head peered down at her, breathing fire so close the Scathach smelled her own singed hair and sniffed burned lace. With both hands, she circled herself with a ring of fire, and the dragon drew back; then the giant she-beast saw the small bullock sleeping peacefully by Maeve's clothes. The Scathach threw a ring of fire around the little animal but not before the dragon had scorched his furry ear—the little bull jumped in the air and bawled at the top of his young voice.

"Hush, you silly fool. Down," the Scathach commanded

fiercely and Little Brown crumpled in a terrified heap. The dragon writhed in the heavens and peered down at her again.

She clapped her hands with joy.

"Oh, wonder beast, one does not see thy skin tacked to the walls of the dwellings of man, nor yet used as a rug! Oh, yes, Young One, you are worth preserving—you can preserve yourself!"

For an instant, the Scathach admired the magnificent beast. Fire belched from the dragon's mouth so high it looked like a burning tree, the long gleaming tail circling around the rocks and out of sight. The Scathach said, "Enough." She tossed dust on the fire, and the dragon vanished, the sky dark and quiet where she had been, and Maeve was asleep again in her place by the fire.

Little Brown still had his eyes wide and he bleated a low, "Aa-aa-aa—" The Scathach, her eyes small pebbles again, fixed a glare on him. "Silly beast, sleep." Little Brown fell over as if struck on the skull and slept.

The Scathach saw the first pale light over the tops of the rocks, not dawn, but its first messenger. She stretched her old bones and looked at the sleeping girl on the bare earth. She ran her stubby fingers up and down the front of the fur vest and touched the rich lace of Maeve's kerchief on her head. She chuckled with mischief. She walked to the side of the stream and sat down on the bank. She lowered her feet into the water and a shiver ran through her body from toes to head. She waited, squinching up her face, then she slid into the water, her head disappearing slowly, then the last of the white lace melted into the low white mist and the surface of the water was without a ripple.

* * *

The sun drifted through the snowy mists of morning in spots like buttercups. Maeve awoke with a soft nuzzling on her ear, then a rough tongue dragged lovingly across her face. Startled, she opened her eyes, laughed, and rolled away from the little bull. She sat up and hugged him. "Oh, Little Brown, you are well." She shivered. "What happened to my fur vest? Brrrrr. You are nice and warm—you had my cloak. I am ice."

Then Maeve unclasped the silver medallion, the royal crest of her family, from her collar. She tore a strip from her skirt, and fastening the silver medallion on it, she made a leash for Little Brown and placed it loosely around his neck.

"You are not leading me on a merry chase again, Little One. No." With one hand holding the leash, she reached down for the cloak and whipped it in the air to rid it of ashes and dust. Then she threw it over her shoulders. Little Brown tugged at the silver-studded halter, but Maeve stood gazing at the black ashes of the fire.

"I feel I had a dream that was a marvel, a great wonder —I cannot capture the memory. . . ." Little Brown tugged again, starting to bawl with hunger.

"Perhaps it will return to me, that dream—yes, we will go home."

They began the long trudge back to Teltown, with Maeve Moira searching the rocks and hummocks for her kerchief of white lace and her long vest of fur.

2.

Maeve Gwenna – Twelfth Century

In such a world as this, one expects that
women should be something more than human and gods
something less than divine.

R. A. Breatnach,
Irish Sagas
Radio Eireann

Wherein Maeve Moira's descendants have migrated to Brennith, England. Maeve Gwenna's person and property are under a hateful guardianship. The Scathach, being a shape shifter, has taken the form of a great eagle. She flies with Maeve Gwenna to the tip of Wales. The young woman is left there to make her new life close to a village of stranded Vikings.

The wings of the great eagle glinted in the sun as she soared over the hamlet. Her eyes caught the movement of a speckled grouse scurrying in the blackthorn miles away; that was her natural vision.

With her supernatural vision—when her marvelous eyes turn as green as emeralds—she can see back in time and forward in time: watch the centuries marching by in review and into the future, that future that is unknown to humans.

In the hamlet below her, the folk, as well as the monks in the nearby abbey, prepared for the Feast of St. Edmund. The bells from the abbey trembled on the air, starlike and pure. The eagle's wingspan cast a shadow far below as she glided toward the river. When she saw the silver gleam of a salmon under the surface of the water, she plummeted, grasping the fish with her talons. Water sparkled on the tips of her primary feathers as she rose with grace into the sky; in her claws dangled the salmon.

Above the crackling of the kitchen fire, Maeve Gwenna heard the sound of a horse shaking his brass trappings and pawing the cobbles with his forefeet. She knew it would be Hericourt, her betrothed, and she did not want to see him. She wiped her hands on her apron and prepared to flee. To her guardian's wife she said quickly, "Madame, I go for more blackberries," and hastened through the kitchen door. Her glossy red hair she covered with her shawl, lest a glimpse of it reveal her hiding place.

When Maeve Gwenna reached the edge of the oak wood, she heard Hericourt speaking with her guardian.

From among the oaks and aspens, she watched the horseman. He dismounted, his trained hawk fluttering on his raised arm. As the sun colored his face, his fine aristocratic bones were defined as if chiseled. She could not see Hericourt's eyes from where she hid but she knew them well enough: blue, blue as crystal-clear sky, and cold, cold as stream water in winter.

The hawk on his arm bated—hung upside down, beating its wings pitifully. Then she knew Hericourt's errand. He had trained his hawks to hunt for prey too large, foxes and wolves, for sport. The hawks were often damaged, if not killed. He could well do the feather work himself, but no, he brought the poor hurt creatures to her. His impatient fingers would not give the feathers the time and skill the work required. Worse, it gave him an excuse to see her.

Maeve Gwenna leaned her head against the rough oak bark.

A fool am I. He needs no excuse.

Her guardian made all the decisions about her life and her property. He had chosen Hericourt. That cruel heart which cared not for the pain of his birds and those cold blue eyes belonged to the man who would be her husband.

Maeve did not know that many others had sought her hand, and not only because of her property. With her fiery hair that glowed like embers in the sun, green eyes flecked with amber and her ivory skin, she caught the eye of male and female alike, young and old, and news of her beauty had traveled far afield. But her guardian gave no thought to the character or suitability of the man he chose for her: Hericourt owned the most property and his alliance with Maeve would increase the guardian's wealth and power.

Maeve was helpless to change the marriage contract, but to the anger of her guardian, she vanished into hiding, as she did now in the wood, to avoid Hericourt whenever possible.

The familiar whirring of wings over her head told her that her own falcon, Fiona, had found her hiding place. She raised her wrist for the bird to alight.

"Oh, Fiona, you will give away my hiding place. I should

have left you jessed. You wouldn't want that handsome dolt to find me, would you now?"

But even as she spoke, she stroked the bird on the wings and throat.

"Come, Fiona, on my shoulder. I left to gather blackberries and gather blackberries I must, or my guardian's wife will turn my face as red as Parthian leather with the back of her hand."

At that moment, a crash and a tumult—a thrashing, then a scream—came through the tree; leaves scattered, branches overhead lashed and shook.

Maeve Gwenna dropped her basket and Fiona quivered on her shoulder, digging her sharp little talons into Maeve's neck.

A great eagle floundered in the tree, her wings caught. Two of her primary feathers drifted down through the leaves as Maeve watched with horror the bird's writhing among the branches.

"Oh, poor creature! And so beautiful and big she is!"

Leaves fell as in a snowstorm as the eagle became more entangled, hopelessly struggling and trapped.

"Stop. Stop," called Maeve, as if the huge bird could understand. "Why did you dive into a tree, majestic fool?"

Stepping up into the crotch of the oak, Maeve pulled herself up to see better. Fiona trembled, curling into the curve of Maeve's neck.

Something cold and wet flopped into Maeve's upturned face—the salmon the eagle had caught—then the fish slid down the front of Maeve's apron to the earth.

Pushing back the leaves, Maeve exclaimed, "Ah, Fiona,

she is jessed with a red leather thong. She must be the eagle of the king—only royalty is allowed to train an eagle!"

The leather thong dangled low enough for Maeve, teetering, to grab it. When she tugged on the jess, the big bird calmed, ceased beating its magnificent wings and grasped a thick branch with her talons. Large and green was the eye she turned on Maeve. Fiona snuggled under Maeve's hair and kept herself out of sight of that emerald eye.

Maeve said, "I will have to hood you to imp those feathers you lost, my friend, or you will not be able to fly back to your royal master."

She climbed down and scrabbled through the fallen leaves until she found the wing feathers the great bird had damaged. On top of a blanket of leaves, she placed them in the blackberry basket, then she hurried toward the house. The silhouette of Hericourt riding away gladdened her heart.

When she reached the courtyard, she saw the angry face of her guardian and from there she looked into the angry face of his wife. They knew she had slipped away from Hericourt. She slowed her steps. Then, thinking of the eagle, she lifted her head and almost managed to avoid their slaps as she dodged into the hawkery.

Maeve's feet in the low-slung stone building stirred the fuzz like snowflakes from the many birds that had housed there. Larger feathers, ones that could be used for imping wings, protruded from clay jars in neat order. Small pots held powder for imping and others were filled with ointment for damaged eyes. The smell was slightly sweet and yet rank from the leather strips to be made into jesses for trained birds. Hooks on the wall held different sized hoods, but none of them would be large enough for so huge an eagle.

Hastily, Maeve made a makeshift sack to hood the eagle, and leaving Fiona jessed in the hawkery, returned to the tree where the great bird perched. The eagle was quiet, her startling green eyes closed.

"What good fortune," Maeve murmured to herself, climbing the oak quietly. She would have to get higher than the eagle's head to drop the hood over because she did not want to chance being torn by the creature's sharp talons.

The task was surprisingly easy. The eagle's eyes did not open as Maeve climbed from limb to limb, higher and higher, and when she was above the eagle, she dropped the hood lightly over its head. Then she breathed easily and gazed down from her own high perch.

From that vantage point almost at the top of the tree, she looked at the surrounding territory below. She could see the neat golden layers of reeds on the monastery stables and the manure collector with his cart of rude brown manure. She watched laborers digging for chalk in a rough field and—No! Hericourt, her betrothed, she saw again approaching in the direction of her guardian's manor house.

Her hands covered her face, and she spoke aloud, forgetting where she was, the eagle, everything—"Oh, grief chokes me and my heart burns within me. I raven in spirit —I cannot raven in word or deed except in secret—but I raven, I raven—"

"Oh, have done with ravening and heart burning, and the grief choking as well," said an old cracked voice.

Maeve's eyes flew wide and she looked everywhere for the speaker.

There was no one.

"Cease falling about in the tree and take this cursed thing from my head," the voice crackled again.

Maeve's eyes now jerked toward the eagle. As she watched, astonished, her whole scalp tickled with terror.

Through the leather bag, the green eyes of the eagle glowed like green fire.

The bird spoke, "Have your wits left you or is it only your ears? Take this thing off me."

Maeve gingerly reached out and lifted the hood from the bird's head, clutching the sack to her body as if to protect herself.

"Lost your speech, have you, since you've heard mine? That is well. I shall leave you unable to speak for a moon or two. If you cannot speak, it will keep you from telling secrets." The eagle cackled wickedly to herself. "Your stilled tongue will also relieve me from listening to your ravening, grief choking and heart burning."

Maeve was motionless, staring in awe and fright, not fear that the eagle would harm her with her claws, but fear of what she knew was present with her in the high leaves of that oak; she knew it was magic. Yes, magic—but was it good or evil? And did the eagle really have the magic power to keep Maeve from speaking?

The eagle peered down through the leaves, then said, "Gather those blackberries. You can fix my feathers anon —I crave a blackberry tart or two."

I dream, Maeve thought as she descended from the tree, *I dream that when my feet touch ground, I will awake.*

Just as her feet touched ground, she saw the silvery fish lying on the fallen leaves.

The eagle's voice croaked, "Make haste—and take that salmon to the cook—I despise raw fish."

The salmon was smoking slowly on the stone hearth when Maeve's guardian and his wife returned from vespers at the abbey. Just as they reached the gate, the eagle, dragging one wing for balance, hobbled across the stones to the kitchen window. She dug her beak into one of the juicy blackberry tarts.

"E-e-e-yi-ii!" the wife screamed in rage, rushing at the bird with her riding whip.

The eagle continued gobbling the tart until the wife, with whip raised, was almost upon her. Then the big bird turned, stretched her splendid wings full length and flapped; dust and debris whirled in the courtyard in a sudden storm. The bird's eyes blazed; she opened her keen-edged beak and gave a high-pitched shriek.

The wife toppled in terror into her husband's arms. He chided her, saying, "Woman, that's the king's bird, surely. It has a jess on the leg—and has lost feathers—let Maeve see to it—Maeve!" he ended in a shout.

He steered his wife in a wide circle away from the eagle who was now hissing furiously.

Maeve ran from the hawkery when she heard the scream; now she approached the eagle slowly. At the sight of her, the bird lowered her wings and closed her beak. Still, Maeve was wary.

"Repair those feathers, Maeve," her guardian ordered. To his wife, he said, "Perchance we shall be rewarded by the king."

Maeve would have cooed soothing words to the bird, but

26

her power of speech was gone. Instead, she stroked the eagle's feathers, and the bird followed her to the fringe of trees.

"Not a bad blackberry tart," the eagle murmured in a low voice, "but what a screech-bag, that woman."

Then the eagle chuckled and said, "She is on her knees saying the rosary right now—and will be for nine days—from the fright I gave her." Maeve broke into laughter, then sobered and stared at the eagle reproachfully because she could not speak.

The bird said, "Fret not, Little One. You will speak again in time. Best, for now, that your tongue does not flap."

Maeve heaved a deep sigh—that was all she could do, and then ran back to get the feathers and powder for replacing the eagle's primaries. When she returned, she set about her work with deft fingers.

At last the feathers were back in place. Maeve sat on her heels, pleased. The eagle did not open her eyes or move. When Maeve started to walk away, the eagle spoke. "Now get a brychan—for padding, as my back is bony—and a blanket for warmth—we leave tonight."

Maeve faced her in blank astonishment, her eyes wide and her mouth gaping.

"And bring that silver medallion your grandmother gave you when you were a child. . . ." Maeve, motionless, continued to stare.

"Go, woman. That handsome oaf, Hericourt, is not the mate for you nor is he the only one who wears a codpiece. This hamlet, Brennith, will be laid bare by the plague—the Black Death—the streets will be littered with more dead bodies than there are villagers to remove them; there will be *no* Brennith in two hundred years...."

Maeve began to laugh. Did the eagle think she would live two hundred years?

The eagle shook her head and the feathers on her neck rose in a ruff of irritation. "Don't be shortsighted! Your descendants—your children's children—your daughters! I must protect them, too—now, go—we leave at midnight—"

Maeve's hand flew to her mouth and her eyes were fearful, but she walked obediently into the twilight.

When she returned, she brought a rolled brychan, a blanket and the scrollwork medallion, too black with tarnish to show the silver.

The eagle commanded her to rub the medallion with wool. This she did with the hem of her skirt—and the metal shone, shimmered—bright silver. The lacy scrollwork revealed the design of a crest.

"Wear it," commanded the eagle. "It has belonged to Maeves for hundreds of years."

With wonder, Maeve turned the silver medallion over in her fingers and then pinned it at her throat.

The bird spoke again. "Come back at midnight."

Suddenly, Maeve shook her head violently and her lips trembled. She tugged on the eagle's wing.

The great bird eyed her impatiently.

"What ails you now? You cannot regret leaving that cruel pair of guardians!"

Maeve shook her head "no" but beckoned the eagle to follow. The eagle, graceful in the heavens, but clumsy on the earth, straggled after her.

In a shallow pen in the courtyard were two sheep. Maeve dropped to her knees and buried her face in the neck of the ewe. If she could talk, she would tell the eagle the many times she had bleached the neck of that sheep with her tears. She would say that she had nurtured both ram and ewe from quivering lambs.

At St. Etherelda's fair, among the monks and merchants, she made a trade for her sheep with a young bronzed shepherd. He bartered for Maeve's handwoven cloak, embroidered with purple thread, dyed with berries picked by Maeve's own hand. He wanted it for his bride, and though the cloak had been two years' labor for Maeve, she desired the two lambs so much she made the trade. One tiny wooly body she wrapped in her shawl, the other in her silk kerchief, and bare-armed and bareheaded, she fairly ran home with her lovable burden.

I have sung them all the songs of my heart, both merry and sad, thought Maeve. How can I part with them? And the ewe's first lamb? What if she needs me?

The eagle was silent, watching as both sheep nuzzled Maeve's face and rubbed against her neck. They were rugged upland sheep, too lean for the best mutton, but with the longest fleeces for making fine wool. The ewe's body swelled; she was carrying her first lamb.

The eagle said, "Aye, they may come. By chance, they might be useful," and as Maeve kissed their shaggy heads and jumped up smiling, the bird continued, "but they will *walk!* Long it will be—over mountains—that falcon of yours, she can lead them." Suddenly, she ruffled her feathers and growled with impatience. "Now, go. *Nothing else.* I wait."

29

They left at midnight, soaring into a night so black Maeve could only feel, not see, the feathered neck she clung to. Yet the skin of her face told her they were rising higher and higher as wind brushing against her exposed cheek became tepid, cool, cold, and then bitterly biting icy. She would have shivered from the temperature, but she already trembled with excitement and fear.

All evening before leaving, she had swung from anger at the bird for taking her voice, to trust in the bird as a magical protector, back to fury that she was being captured—almost—from the only home she knew; then joy at escaping from a life where she was powerless to direct her own destiny.

The eagle is concerned with the Black Death, Maeve thought, and my children. But without Hericourt, I shall *have* neither sons nor daughters.

And how did she know my ancient grandmothers, Maeve puzzled—this wondrous bird—and about the silver medallion the women in my heritage have handed down until it came to me?

These questions roiled in Maeve's brain again as they sped through night with mists blacking out the stars, as dark above as it was below; finding no answers, her head drooped at last and she slept on the eagle's back, protected from falling by the protruding wing sockets.

Fire colors streaked the sky when Maeve opened her eyes. Looking down, she saw the rising sun's reflection on glassy sparkling lakes and streams, on dew-covered rooftops; diamonds, with facets of ruby and sapphire, glittered on the trees. Black peaks of mountains poked up toward her with green sweeping valleys between them. Looking up, she saw ribbons of blue sky through lavender and rose clouds. The magnificence astonished her; she felt her spirits flying as the eagle was flying—and she knew: This is the life of a bird.

Oh, how fortunate, she thought. Fiona, my friend, I never envied you before. Why do you ever return to earth?

But to earth they did return, just at the moment Maeve glimpsed the whitecaps on the ocean and morning smoke fires rising slowly from a village far below.

The eagle settled gently in huge boulders on a cliff. Looking down, down, down the steep cliff, Maeve saw more clearly the gleaming ocean and specks who must be villagers walking about their morning chores.

The eagle said, "We wait for darkness. If you are seen riding on an eagle's back, the Vikings in the village will burn you for a witch." When the eagle finished speaking, she stretched her long neck and preened her feathers.

Vikings? Maeve's eyes widened in horror. Tales of Vikings had been handed down from the Celtic side of her family as long as she could remember. They were told beside the hearth on stormy nights like ghost stories that left the listeners huddled together and shivery—with good reason. Savage Vikings came in their ships and looted everything valuable to carry away with them. What was left they burned to the ground: crops in the fields, buildings, and stored seed, leaving the Celts to starve. Maeve could hear the distant voice of her grandmother telling the grisly tale.

Maeve's face clearly registered her horror and the eagle turned one fierce eye on her again. "Come now. These Vikings have been stranded for years. They tend their sheep and grow their meager patches of food just as the folk in

31

Brennith." Then she chuckled low in her throat. "But they do not cross the mountains because of their misdeeds long ago."

Maeve's mouth set in a firm line and her eyes grew hard with determination. No matter what the eagle said, they were evil savage people and she would have nothing to do with them. She vowed to herself that she would die of loneliness first. And when she had her two sheep—and here she smiled—and her new baby lamb, she would have all the friends she needed. If she climbed back up this high cliff, she would be able to see them making progress across the valleys on the other side.

As if the bird could read her mind, she spoke harshly. "Come not back to the cliff. *Come not.* A wild hermit lives here among the rocks. You must protect yourself and survive."

Maeve, seated on a granite rock, looked around her with wide eyes.

A wild hermit?

She saw no signs of human life, only bird droppings and scattered feathers of hundreds of roosting seagulls and cormorants. She swallowed hard and tried to hide her quivering hands behind her brown woolen skirt.

The bird spoke more kindly. "You are from a bloodline of women with courage and wits. You must use your spirit. I will *not* come back to help you."

Then the big bird shuddered, exhausted from her flight. Maeve saw it and, ashamed to be so thoughtless, quickly unwrapped a copper bowl from her brychan. She placed cold salmon wrapped in watercress and blackberry tarts on a white cloth. With her dirk, she sliced cold mutton and cut thick pieces of cheese.

The smell of food opened the eagle's greedy eyes. Without a word, she gobbled most of everything while Maeve nibbled a piece of bread and cheese and a corner of a tart. Then the bird slept and Maeve, lying on her stomach, watched the tiny black specks in the hamlet far below. Knowing they were Vikings made her heart race with fear. She could not even explain herself with speech. And the sheep. Looking down, it seemed a mile straight down to the beach. How would they ever traverse that steep cliff?

On closer inspection, flat ledges connected into each other in a way that would make climbing down possible, but the descent would be tortuous and difficult. Also, it would take the sheep a long time to cross the valleys, rivers, and mountains that the eagle had flown in one night. Maeve sighed. It would be so lonely without the sheep and Fiona.

As darkness fell, the eagle stirred. Maeve stuck the knife in her belt and wrapped the copper bowl in her brychan. At last, the dark below was complete, except for one glowing fire.

"Shepherds," said the eagle as they left the cliff.

They descended silently through the air, hearing no sound except the ocean surf. The eagle landed with a soft swish of wings, and Maeve's feet touched the sand of her new life.

As silently as she had arrived, the eagle vanished into the black night. Maeve stood facing the sound of the ocean, feeling already the damp wind brushing her face and the cold seeping through the soles of her shoes.

What madness, she thought angrily. The eagle, with her magic, could have made me a shelter ... or ... or left me a pig to roast ... or ...

Voices interrupted her thoughts. The shepherds! Against the embers of the fire, she saw silhouettes of two figures rising, their staves in their hands, and they set off into the dark. Now with her eyes more accustomed, Maeve saw the shell of a hut, a wall gone on one side and with only half a roof—shelter, nonetheless. She smiled to herself. Had the eagle left her shelter, after all? She crept to the shepherd's fire and with her brychan picked up two of the warm stones. Then she scooped up hot coals in her copper bowl.

Maeve stumbled on the floor of the hut: dirt and rocks. In the most sheltered corner, she set down the bowl of embers. Then she cocooned herself into the brychan with the warm rocks. Whatever the morrow brings, she thought, I shall sleep warm this night—even if it is my last; and she drifted into sleep, dreaming that she saw her sheep on the high cliff making their way down to her, Fiona fluttering above them like an angel.

The gray dawn came, a lemony sun appeared through the mists of the ocean, and at last the sky was a brilliant clear blue and the sun a round hot ball. Maeve slept on but she had pushed her brychan away from her face and shoulders as the day became warmer. Her red hair splayed across the brown brychan like flames; her long golden eyelashes brushed her cheeks colored peach by the sunshine.

She awoke to the sound of footsteps crunching in the gravelly pebbles outside and blinked into the noon sunshine.

Her eyes opened wider as a man's face, blackened except

around the eyes—great blue eyes—appeared at the open wall. She gasped and the face disappeared instantly, even as Maeve's hand flew to the dirk in her belt. Her instinct to protect herself was so quick, she did not really think until she looked down in her hand and saw the dirk's sharp blade gleaming in the sun. Only then did she hear the rapid retreat of the heavy footsteps and saw her own hand trembling.

Why does the barbarian Viking paint his face black with soot? She did not remember her grandmother mentioning that when she told her tales of the seafarers. How strange.

She trembled when she thought of the Viking watching her while she slept. She would always keep her knife in her belt.

To her surprise, the fire, though low, was still flickering pale blue. The embers she had taken from the shepherds' fire must be something other than wood; she knew from Brennith that wood would never burn so long. What could it be? They had none of it in Brennith. Still, it would not burn forever. She must find scraps of wood to keep it going for the chilly night, but she was hungry. Finding food would come first. She went to the beach.

Deep blue green, the water sparkled in the sunshine. The tide was out, leaving pools in the rocks full of warm water and sea creatures; hard-shelled animals with pincers and round spiny sea dwellers. She gathered them in her skirt and, in the shelter, roasted them over the embers, eating every speck. They were tasteless, and her mouth watered for the blackberry tarts of Brennith. Even as she compared the flaky crusts of the pies with the cracked shells of the animals she had eaten, she thought with a sigh, starve I shall not.

At that moment she saw a dumped stack of the black rocks, whatever they were, like the embers she had carried from the shepherd's fire. Soot-Face must have left them while she was at the ocean. She was grateful, but had no intention of being friendly. When her falcon and the sheep arrived, she would have all the companions she needed.

She could not keep from watching the high cliff, and in her mind, seeking a path along the ledges and boulders that the sheep could travel down to her. But they would have only begun their journey; they would only now be picking their way past the green pastures of Brennith. Lonely, she walked back to the beach to find a place to bathe.

The glittering sun, now flecked with foam of the returning tide, fascinated her for she had always lived in the woodland. She gazed, as she bathed, at the magnificent span of ocean as far as the eyes could see. The sun had angled and shone through the rising waves, the color of jade, capped with froth as white as ermine. Sea birds wheeled lazily in the cloudless sky. She smiled, thinking, it *is* a strange and wondrous place.

The days began to fall into a pattern. Each morning Maeve looked up at the cliff first, her eyes searching for the sheep though she knew it was too soon. Soot-Face, bolder, left the long-burning black lumps for her every day from the low cliffs where he dug in the earth for them.

Maeve had seen him one day before he went to his digging and was not yet covered with soot. How different he looked with a rosy face! A young man with good countenance and broad shoulders. A thatch of hair as yellow as butter stuck out from his black woolen cap. His face was rounder than the men of Brennith and lacked their delineated bones. He often smiled at Maeve Gwenna but she was not deceived: He studied the silver medallion at her throat. He meant to steal it and she fingered the dirk at her belt in warning.

Though Maeve saw smoke eddying from the thatched roofs far down the beach, no other villagers came near. She busied herself getting ready for the sheep by cutting the stiffest bushes at the foot of the cliff and wattling them into wicker to thatch more of the roof and to make a pen for the sheep. Her wrists speckled with golden dots from the sun and she thought her face must have also—but she did not much care. She was no longer a lady of Brennith but a woman of her own new world. Only at night, when the wind turned to ice, the rain came down in sheets, and the great waves thundered on the sand as the tide rose to its highest, did she shiver in the corner of the wet shelter and stare out into the blackness. Then the loneliness was almost more than she could bear.

One morning the sky hung heavy with gray clouds almost at the level of the roof and mist curled in through the open wall. The high cliff was shrouded.

If only she were back at the top of the cliff, she could see for miles. She was sure the sheep were in the valleys by now. Yet she remembered that the eagle forbade it because of the hermit. She pondered this thought while she gathered sea creatures to eat. Then she began the tedious task of making wicker, but her thoughts kept returning to the cliff. Finally, she dropped the wattling and rose.

A hermit, after all, is only a man, she argued with herself, and we saw nothing of him when we were on the mountain all day until midnight.

I will go.

Maeve donned her ragged cloak and began the tortuous climb across the ledges and over the rocks to the top of the cliff.

Mists swirled as she crept from shelflike plateaus to narrow ridges of stone; it was late in the day when she reached the crown.

But her heart sank when she reached the place where she and the eagle had rested and had lunch. She was surrounded by fog, a dag so thick she could not see into the valleys below; she could not even see the next mountain. A cold rainy wind sent puffs of fog scudding like dancing ghosts.

Suddenly she tensed, all senses alert. Did she hear something? As if turned to stone, she held her breath to hear better.

A pebble rolled.

She pivoted and searched with her eyes.

Only the gauzy mist drifted, settled, then rose again on the rain-scented breeze.

She breathed again, then thought she saw a dark shadow among the boulders.

She waited. There was nothing more. The cliff was as quiet as if the whole world had vanished and she was the only human left.

And yet, *something* was up there on the top of the cliff with her.

She smelled it—a strong musky animal odor, powerful, primitive, and *near*.

Crouched atop a boulder, a creature completely covered with black fur and wild masses of long dark hair on his head chuffed and grunted like a boar. At first glance, Maeve thought it was half animal, then knew it was the hermit covered with black bear pelt. He stared at her with round black eyes, then crouched lower to lunge.

Terrified, Maeve sprang like a deer, leaping stones, dashing around buttes, sprinting on every flat surface. She saw a dark ravine—a murky split in the rocks. She jumped in, praying there were no animals lurking there. The bottom of the narrow crevice was covered with bird feathers, dropped from thousands of birds. The familiar odor was perfume to Maeve and comfort. She rolled into a tight ball and was absolutely still.

It seemed hours as she grew stiff with cold before she heard the soft rustle of footsteps, no more than a whisper over the rocks—no more sound than the slithering of a snake. Maeve scarce breathed.

A sharpened stick poked into the ravine, stirring feathers, making a cloud that half covered her face. Then the needle-like point of the stick pierced her leg. Pain shot through her calf and she knew from the sudden warmth that she was bleeding. Yet, she was as still and quiet as the stones on which she curled.

Long after the whispering footsteps had gone, Maeve stayed rigid, never moving a muscle, though her leg pained her. When she emerged with aching bones, night had fallen black, and a light rain set her teeth to chattering.

Under cover of darkness, favoring her injured leg, she crawled, never once standing up, never leaving one stone shelf, until, on her hands and knees, she was sure of the next ledge. It took hours. The rain stopped, the gray dawn came and went, and the sun edged coral on the horizon.

At last, she nestled on a ledge close to the foot of the

cliff and rested, letting the sun dry her damp cloak and warm her body. She could see her tattered shelter, and in her relief, it was beautiful. In her heart, it was home.

But her eyes opened wide at something she had not seen before. Close to her shelter, tiny flowers were blooming—a scrollwork etched in lavender, pink, and lemon yellow. It was the design of her medallion. Only Soot-Face could have done that. It must be the hardy little mountain flowers he had transplanted there—when?—and then summer rain and sun had brought them to blossom. It was a thoughtful work of art and the last thing in the world Maeve would have expected from a savage.

Still marveling at the flowers, she inspected her leg where the sharp stick had pierced it. The wound was not deep and the blood had dried. She would soak in the salt water; she started toward the beach.

When she had almost reached the tide pools, on impulse she looked back toward the top of the cliff. Two tiny creatures were silhouetted there, a black speck flying above them. The sheep and Fiona at last!

Maeve ran across the sand, gravel, and rocks and climbed up in the low boulders to wait for them; they grew larger as she watched, painstakingly edging along the treacherous ledges. The ewe, heavy with her lamb, swayed clumsily on the narrow precipices, then stumbled as she followed the ram in small leaps to another boulder. Maeve watched with her hand on her throat. For once, she was glad she couldn't cry out—as she would have—and distract them from their dangerous descent.

The sun of high noon grew hot on the top of Maeve's

head and perspiration rolled on her face—from fear, from heat, and from longing.

Finally, she could really see their shaggy coats, long fine wool, though grimy with dust. Fiona, her feathers glistening, hovered above the sheep. Maeve began to smile, knowing she would soon have them in her arms; she could still hug them, even if she couldn't lift them anymore. She raised her arm for the falcon, and the bird glided gracefully to her shoulder, then curled in the curve of her neck.

At that moment, the ewe tripped and fell.

She bounced with heart-piercing thuds on the boulders below, and rolled into a low cluster of rocks just above the level of Maeve's head. The horror of it stunned Maeve; she was momentarily paralyzed, unbelieving. The ram stopped, motionless, on the ledge, looking down, as if he, too, could not believe it.

Maeve scrabbled, tearing her nails and hands to get up the rocks, clambering and sliding on the loose stones, weeping, shuddering at what she would find. Finally, her hands bleeding, she reached the ewe.

Trickles of blood ran from the sheep's mouth and ears, her head hung limply—crazily—over a boulder's edge. Maeve knelt and gently slipped her arms around her, laying her head on the ewe's upturned chest. The ewe moaned piteously, her breath coming in gasps. Fiona shrieked over their heads but Maeve did not look up. She could hear the ewe's heart beating, and even as she listened, it stopped. She wept all the harder, unable to move.

Maeve was surprised to feel a thump in her own ribs, nestled on the ewe's body. Another thump—she sat up, startled. The lamb! The lamb was alive and kicking. She laid her hand on the ewe and felt the thumps plainly with the palm of her hand.

She placed her hand on the still warm nose of the ewe and tears blurred her vision. "My friend, my dear friend—" Maeve was astonished as she heard her own voice; her speech had returned. "Perhaps I can save your lamb, and then you will live on in your descendants."

With a trembling hand, she drew her knife from her belt, praying that she could do what she had often watched the shepherds in Brennith do. Because she was blinded by tears, she used her sense of touch—the sure touch of her hands— rather than her eyes. One arm covered the kicking lamb that she would not cut where it lay, and the other, holding the dirk, ripped through the tough hide and all the protective coverings until she lifted the small creature from its mother.

Maeve's eyes were blurred and though she could not see the little animal, she could feel its warm body and hear its heart beating when she lowered her ear. She was exhausted, drained, sad, and joyful. Curling the lamb in one arm and covering it with the hem of her skirt, she wiped her face on her skirt as well. The deluge of tears had been stemmed; she brushed her hair back with a sticky hand and now inspected the lamb. *The tiny female needs its mother to wash it with her tongue,* she thought sadly; *and how shall I keep it warm?*

Even at that moment, what had been a zephyr became a wind, rustling the dust into eddies. The ewe's wool. If she sheared her—but where to put the lamb? Only the cold rocks faced her. Holding the lamb in one arm, she tried to stoop to begin shearing, but her balance wavered.

A hand on her arm steadied her. She saw five sooty fingers grasping her forearm. She looked up into the warm blue eyes of Soot-Face. His hands reached out then and took the tiny wet squirming lamb, cradling it in his arms like a human infant. Maeve was too surprised to protest, and from the tender way Soot-Face nestled the baby lamb, no savage was he.

She bent to the work of shearing the ewe with her dirk, not making a thorough job, but getting enough wool to keep the lamb warm. She piled the wool in a big puff, and when she had finished, Soot-Face had already wrapped the little animal in it. Smiling, he handed the newborn back to Maeve.

3.

Maeve Brigitta – Seventeenth Century

Accuse not nature; she hath done her part.
Do thou but thine.

> John Milton,
> *Paradise Lost*

Wherein Maeve Brigitta travels with her trader father from Britain to New France—Canada. Exploring to find a place for a settlement in the wilderness, they are endangered by the Iroquois and the natural elements. The Scathach again keeps her promise to help Maeve's daughters survive.

When the ship *at last* neared the coast of New France, all the stars except Venus had vanished. The pewter gray ocean reflected the soft pinks and blues of dawn. Maeve Brigitta clung to her father's arm on the deck, leaning on the rail. She turned up the collar of her coat against the summer morning damp. Her father, as a trader, had seen the coast many times, but Maeve Brigitta had not, and her eyes were wide with awe.

Trees. The whole land was covered with shades of green: from the palest, through emerald to the darkest, richest deep hunter green. The forest stretched as far as Maeve's eye could see. Then as they navigated the mouth of the river, the white cliffs rose opposite the masses of green, and huge rocks rose from the water. The rocks were so blanketed by birds that the stones appeared to be solid black with moving creatures circling, alighting, rising. Maeve, overwhelmed at the sights, hardly heard the excited gabble of other passengers or noticed the nudges as they all tried to get a view. Her father squeezed her arm and she looked up at his fair skin and blue eyes. He was smiling.

She said in a whisper, "I am so glad you let me come with you. It is more vast and beautiful than I ever dreamed!"

The trader raised an eyebrow. "Untamed is what it is." He pointed to a ship flying the French flag. "And the French are trying to tame it. Our ship carries fine English wool and commodities, but that French ship is loaded with families and 'King's Daughters'."

Maeve Brigitta's eyes blinked.

"How many daughters does the French king *have*?" she asked in wonder.

"They are not really daughters of the king. They are orphans or widows or girls raised in the workhouse. They have no dowries with which to get married." Her father gazed at the banks of the St. Lawrence River as they sailed toward Quebec. "That leaves them no choice except the convent. But the king has furnished them with an alternative to suit his purpose. He has endowed them with the household properties they will need and also dowries to help colonize New France."

48

"I have heard of women being shipped to the colonies, but rumor was that they were street strumpets."

"*No*. The only women allowed to be 'King's Daughters' have to be religious and of high moral character. They have to be healthy and skilled in homemaking. They are expected to help the Jesuit missionaries or be wives and mothers."

Maeve was filled with curiosity about the "King's Daughters." "What courage they must have! I shall be interested to see these women who cross the ocean alone and become a wife to anyone who claims them."

Her father looked at her thoughtfully. "The women themselves have the final choice. The interested man and the woman sign with the notary. Then they have a chance to talk to each other . . ." he chuckled, "under the sharp eyes of the Ursuline nuns. But they can break that contract at any time, and sign with another person until they both are agreeable. Only then do they marry."

He motioned to Maeve to look back at the French ship. "You can watch the 'King's Daughters' disembark as we will put into the quay before they do."

And so Maeve watched the "King's Daughters" take their first tread on new soil. And she was not alone. Lofty officials, Jesuit priests, middle-class people, artisans, and colonists hastened to welcome them, these daughters of France. The women were of a variety of ages, certainly not all young girls, and they were charmingly dressed in close-fitting coats of camlet over farradine skirts, taffeta hoods, and each of them had a lawn handkerchief in her hand. Most of them looked solemn, understandably, facing a whole new world, but Maeve caught the eye of a girl with flashing black eyes whose dark curls were springing from her hood. Maeve smiled

49

at her and she returned a dimpled merry grin. Maeve's French was not extensive, but she edged through the crowd to speak to the girl. Before she had a chance, two formidable Ursuline nuns gathered the group of "King's Daughters" and hustled them off to the convent.

And Maeve was hustled off to the governor's compound by her father, as the narrow streets of Quebec were crowded with sailors and trappers who ogled any woman, much more a beautiful young one with unusual red hair.

During some of her father's trading negotiations, Maeve was allowed to join him. Then she had a chance to see the houses and citizens of Quebec. Once she saw two Indians —swarthy countenances they had, and ungroomed hair. And she saw again the little "King's Daughter" she had seen on the wharf. As it turned out, she was invited to the girl's wedding.

"So soon?" exclaimed Maeve when her father told her.

"Yes, she and a French trapper named Bompie signed with the notary, had two conversations, and are ready to get married. And they are coming with our group. They want to settle outside the seigneury." Her father straightened the cravat he was wearing to the wedding. "I know Bompie from summers before and he is a free-spirited young man. He wouldn't do well in the strict religious rule of a township." At Maeve's questioning glance, he continued. "Oh, he's re-liable as a rock—and laughs easily. Two good qualities in the wilderness. That young woman will have no regrets."

Though it was a warm summer day, Maeve added a light blue linen jacket to her brown dress to look nicer for the wedding. "Who else is going up the river?"

Her father opened the door as he answered. "There will

be twenty of us. Fewer than that would not be safe. I need to find four more men. The rest of them will be at the wedding." He laughed. "Bompie invited everybody, friends and strangers."

"Wait," Maeve said suddenly. She ran back, found her silver medallion in the trunk and pinned it on her jacket.

When she took his arm, her father said, "You look so pretty, I shall be besieged to let some man sign with you at the notary. And then he will be underfoot all the time until you decide to marry!"

"Oh, stop jesting, Father!" But she blushed.

The wedding in the chapel was simple and serious. Maeve was strangely touched by the sight of the small bride wearing the same clothes she wore when she left the ship. Bompie was short and husky with wild dark hair he had tried to slick down for the ceremony. It still stuck up in the back like a rooster tail. Of the guests, Maeve was among the best dressed, as these were working people, not the aristocrats from "Uppertown." But there was one tall, distinguished-looking man who was elegantly dressed in light brown: a velvet waistcoat and matching britches with gleaming leather boots the color of chestnuts. His black beard had certainly not been trimmed by woodsman's scissors.

"Who is that?" Maeve asked her father.

"Count Rastoff, the Russian. He'll go with our party. The Russians are very interested in beaver fur. We'll meet him at the inn tonight."

At the inn, Maeve met the rest of the party, but the ones she remembered the most were Viette, the bride, and Margarite, a young widow who would help the missionaries, the unforgettable Russian count, and, of course, genial Bompie, whom she liked right away. Two Jesuit priests would travel with them, Father Jean, a muscular stocky fellow who looked like a woodcutter, and Father Daneau, sedate and meditative, a scholar.

When the group gathered the next morning at the break of dawn, their meager belongings had already been divided, with the provisions, between two large canoes. Maeve had hardly slept all night and her father had returned long after midnight. He had been busy finishing all the preparations with Bompie and the other men of the party. Maeve saw several men she had not met.

One young Frenchman with dark curls and dark eyes leaped to help her into the canoe. Maeve thought he was going to climb in after her, but Count Rastoff edged forward and took the seat closest to her. She watched with some amusement as the young man negotiated with a trapper to give up his place in the bow. Grumbling, the trapper moved into the other canoe.

The young Frenchman climbed in and then, boldly, almost as if he wanted everyone to take note of it, he looked over his shoulder and flashed Maeve a triumphant, devilish smile. It was too late to pretend she wasn't watching, but she quickly averted her eyes to the houses along the banks of the St. Lawrence River. It was some moments before she realized the boat was being manned through the swift current and that Count Rastoff was speaking to her.

"I see you are interested in the houses," he said. "You will notice as we get into the wilderness, they are much more like small fortresses."

"Because of the Indians? I understood that they are more friendly now."

"Friendly? Would we have fifteen armed men with us if they were friendly?" He stroked his glossy black beard. "The Algonquins are allies of the French, but the Iroquois are enemies of both."

The count smiled. "But you are neither French nor English. Am I not correct?"

Before Maeve answered, the young Frenchman in the front of the canoe turned around and, grinning, listened to their conversation. Feeling color creep into her face, she watched the water rippling by.

"It was generations ago that one of my ancestral grandmothers, who was Irish, married a Viking—or so the tale goes in my family. My name is a combination of the two, so I suppose it is based on fact."

"I can see it," answered the count, "with your red hair and your fair skin. And you must have the spirit of adventure of the Vikings to think of settling in New France. And your mother?"

Maeve Brigitta sighed. "My mother died last year. My younger sisters and I lived with my aunt. I love my aunt, but my father promised I could come with him on my seventeenth birthday. My father is going to homestead now. And trade furs for your people, of course. He has had enough of seafaring."

"*Trois-Rivières!*" shouted the Frenchman, laughing over his shoulder at Maeve. She turned her attention to the banks of the river and saw some black stone houses with small windows and highly sloping roofs surrounded by a stockade. He gazed directly at Maeve, but spoke loudly to the whole group. "Time for bread and cheese, yes?"

Count Rastoff glared at him. Maeve wanted to laugh.

Instead she nodded her head and held her laughter. The bread and cheese were passed from hand to hand and then a jug of apple cider made its way the length of the canoe. Each person had his or her own drinking vessel, and in the warm summer sun, the drink was welcome.

In the quiet after eating, with the gentle plowing of the canoe, Maeve felt drowsy. Count Rastoff seemed lost in his own thoughts and Maeve certainly did not want to fall asleep on his shoulder. She turned behind her to Father Daneau who was sketching the trees and landmarks. The priest showed her his drawing and said, "This one is for my pleasure. On my last trip to France, I sent maps and drawings for the king's chronicles. Are you interested in trees?"

Maeve gestured toward the forests on both banks of the river. "I have never seen so many and I don't think I could name a one."

Father Daneau began drawing again. "They are my special interest. If there is a paradise of trees, it is New France. I will show you when we reach the land grant."

Finally, stiff and tired and sunburned, they disembarked at Ville St. Marie. Maeve and Margarite were housed with a family and the men camped out. Bompie and Viette stayed with friends. Maeve intended to make friends with the quiet young widow, but Margarite was so long on her knees at prayer that Maeve drifted off to sleep.

While it was still dark, Maeve's father woke her. She dressed sleepily and was given a cup of porridge. She and Margarite made their way back to the river with the men. Count Rastoff was standing beside the canoe. They said good morning to each other. Maeve's father was helping with the other canoe when suddenly, out of the dark into the lantern light, the young Frenchman appeared.

He said to Count Rastoff, "Will you present me to this lady? I wish to speak with her."

Count Rastoff frowned. After a moment, he said, "Perhaps you should talk to her father about that."

The Frenchman smiled into the count's scowl. "Did *you*? New France is not the Russian court. I will speak to her father when I ask his permission to marry her. Right now I only want to converse."

Maeve's mouth had dropped in surprise at the brashness of the man. She was speechless.

Count Rastoff hesitated, then slowly he said, "This is Gabriel de Chombray." The count started to take Maeve's hand to help her, but Gabriel reached across him and, taking her arm, assisted her into the canoe. Then he plopped into the place the count had occupied the day before.

He looked up innocently into the count's outraged face. "I cannot talk to her if I'm in the bow of the boat, can I?"

The count regarded him sourly for a moment, but Gabriel busied himself with the oars. The count sat in the bow.

As soon as the boat was in the middle of the river and the sky was showing tinges of pink, Gabriel, managing his paddle expertly all the while, said, "I am going to marry you."

Maeve's eyes opened wide in an indignant stare. In a low furious voice, she said, "I did not come here to seek a husband!"

Gabriel said, "Good. You have no need to seek. He is already found."

Immediately, Maeve turned her head away from Gabriel

and gazed at the riverbank. She thought she heard a chuckle from behind her, but when she looked, Father Daneau was calmly sketching.

To her surprise, something dangled from a tree over the river. As they drew nearer, she saw that it was buffalo robes.

"Father Daneau, what is that?"

Gabriel answered. "The Indians hung it there as an offering to the spirit of the river."

Maeve asked no more questions.

The canoe, borne on the tranquil current, glided in the shade of gray crags festooned with honeysuckle, by trees mantled with wild grapevines, dells bright with flowers of white euphorbia, blue gentian, and purple balm. Matted forests arose where red squirrels leaped and chattered. The noble spruce trees lifted above the others like spires, the lowest branches sweeping almost to earth, then turning up at the tips like fingers lifted in a gesture of grace. The quiet itself was majestic. Maeve was reverent in this cathedral of the wild.

Gabriel's voice interrupted her thoughts. "You should know something about me since we are going to be married."

When he received no answer, he said, "I hate fish."

Father Daneau laughed. "Why do you hate fish, my son?"

"I summered here with my father at the fish-drying quays. We flayed, smoked and dried thousands of pounds of fish to be shipped back to Catholic France. I always smelled of fish. It was on my hands and my clothes and in my hair! I could not get the smell off. I vowed I would never eat fish again. It sickens me."

Father Daneau clucked his tongue. "A man in Quebec

ate meat on Friday and was punished by being fined a cow, one hundred livres, and was placed in the stock in the middle of 'Lowertown' for three hours! Pray tell me, what do you eat on Fridays, as a good French Catholic?"

Gabriel grinned. "That is why I love New France. The Church allows beaver as an amphibian."

Maeve's neck was aching from being cramped so far to the left to avoid talking to Gabriel. She eased her head by looking straight forward.

Gabriel spoke to her again. "I am a carpenter now, as well as a cabinetmaker. I apprenticed to Etienne Giffard in Quebec. He is the best. I am a woodcutter, too. So you see, I can cut trees for clearing, and build you a house, and then carve fine furniture. Ah, the lovely beautiful fine woods we have in New France. Isn't that so, Father?"

"Yes, truly, it is. And Gabriel, did you not serve in the French army?"

"Yes, Father." He spoke to Maeve Brigitta. "And with distinction. I am a good marksman. I can protect you from the Iroquois. I am good-natured and jovial. I love children. I have manners at table." He paused for breath. "And I am not bad looking in my uniform—and when my beard is shaved and my hair is combed!"

Maeve turned toward him. He was grinning mischievously.

She said, "With all those fine qualities, what a pity that you lack one so badly needed."

His dark eyes lighted with a merry amber glint. "And what is that?"

"Modesty," she answered.

Father Daneau burst out laughing and Gabriel did, too,

their laughter falling across the quiet water like dropped pebbles. Maeve could not keep a straight face and at the sudden outburst from the three, the others in the canoe turned around and stared. Maeve tried to appear ladylike and innocent under Count Rastoff's fierce gaze, but she was thinking that Gabriel was far from bad looking even without his dark curly hair combed.

That evening, they landed at Bompie's land grant.

The summer before, he and Gabriel, with other men, had made a small clearing and built a crude cabin. Now they unloaded the canoes and brought them ashore, built a fire for cooking supper, and posted two of the men as armed guards. Maeve was among the first to roll into her furs to go to sleep, while others still talked, making plans around the fire. Her father was engaged with the men, but he hurried in and kissed her cheek. He said, "What do you think of our untamed land?"

"I am glad to be here," she answered.

The next morning, by the time Maeve remembered where she was, the steady *chop* of axes could be heard. The sun was not up, but Viette was, tending the fire and turning meat on a spit. Margarite, Father Daneau, and Father Jean were holding Mass under one of the huge trees. All the men were cutting except Count Rastoff. He and the two Russian servants he had brought with him acted as armed guards. It was to be the pattern of every summer morning. Viette always had the fire blazing and meat cooking by the time Maeve awoke. The religious were already at their prayers. With the twenty of them together, each having his or her own tin bowl and utensil, they served themselves.

Soon another rough cabin was standing. It would be protection for the summer. Then they started the third.

Viette worked constantly. If she was not cooking, she was washing Bompie's clothes, or anyone's, and hanging them on the trees. Maeve helped, but she felt like a sloth beside the busy Viette. The little bride aired the bed skins, helped the men skin the animals they shot, scaled fish, and dried them when they had more than they could eat. She seemed to have irrepressible high spirits. She hummed while she worked and would often break into singing French songs while she washed. Viette and Bompie seemed well matched. They both had a ready laugh. Around the fire at night, tired as they both must have been, they were the two who always started the singing and the men, Margarite, and the priests would join in the folk songs. Maeve, not knowing the songs of France, felt left out, but her father sat on one side and Gabriel promptly ousted anyone who tried to sit on the other side, so she was not lonely.

When the two other cabins, though roughly thrown together, were finished, firewood was stacked against all the inside walls.

"That will serve as a fortress," Gabriel explained.

"But why? There are no Indians about," Maeve said.

Gabriel laughed. "You have not known what you've seen. They can blend with trees and bushes. There is a small band of Iroquois camped not far from our clearing. As long as we show strength, they will keep their distance. They have seen our guns."

Maeve shivered. "What about when Father and Bompie and the men go to trade for furs?"

"Don't worry. We will still be twelve. That is enough. We

will stay closer to the settlement after they have gone upriver."

As the last logs were split for the stockade, Maeve's father and the others loaded the articles for trade with the Algonquins—guns, ammunition, knives, hatchets, kettles, beads, bells, trinkets, and brandy, which had become indispensable to the Indians. On the evening before they canoed upriver, Maeve's father walked with her in the moonlight. The others sat by the fire or finished their preparations for the journey. Bompie and Viette were also outside, sitting on a low limb, and their whispers drifted through the still night.

Maeve's father said, "We will be back by end of summer and return to Quebec for the winter. Next summer, since we have now cleared some fields, we can plant—if you decide to stay in New France."

"I will stay," Maeve answered quickly.

"You have not seen the winter yet, my daughter. But did I notice young Gabriel getting your undivided attention?"

Maeve started to joke, then changed her mind. "He *does* have my undivided attention. What do you think of him?"

"I think there is not a better man in New France." He spoke firmly, then hesitated and continued. "But there will be parties, dances, banquets, and balls in Quebec this winter attended by aristocrats, officers, dukes, counts—you can choose from many."

Maeve said quietly, "I think I have chosen."

They walked back toward the fire. Her father said, "I leave you in good hands. Father Daneau will stay and Father Jean travels with us—"

He was interrupted by a *whoop* from the trappers around the fire. Bompie had appeared with an almost finished cradle.

The tiny cradle announced to all that the first baby of the settlement was on its way. Everyone hastened to congratulate Bompie and Viette. Maeve heard Bompie's hurdy-gurdy playing long after she went to bed.

After the traders departed, Viette moved into Maeve's cabin, and two of the men sometimes slept in the second room. Margarite, Father Daneau, and Gabriel shared the middle cabin, and Count Rastoff and his two servants slept in the third. Often the men slept outside in the summer night. They were accustomed to it and liked building their own fires under the starry skies. They also stood guard.

Maeve found that Viette was a charming companion. At night, the young wife still stayed busy sewing baby clothes, embroidering, making each scrap of cloth count, each minute into a useful occupation. On one of their first nights together, she proudly showed Maeve the properties she was given as a "King's Daughter." It was ordinary clothing, a small money box, a hood, two lawn kerchiefs, shoe ribbons, one hundred sewing needles, a comb, white thread, a pair of stockings, a pair of gloves, scissors, two knives, a thousand pins, a bonnet, four braids, and two livres in silver coin.

It seemed a small amount to Maeve, but Viette's face glowed as if she were wealthy.

"Also, for our household, we received fifty livres in Canadian money for provisions, but we left that in Quebec until we return next summer. We will need seed to plant," Viette said.

"And you will have the baby then, too," said Maeve.

"Yes, I am making the clothes now." She ran her hand over the cradle lovingly. "This is a beautiful country."

"Where was your home in France?"

"I had no home in France. I am an orphan. I grew up in the workhouse. There was never enough food and what we had was the cheapest and worst. In Paris, a stream of sewage ran down the middle of the street." She wrinkled her nose. "It smelled, oh, how it smelled. And the noise, the shouting, the horses, the crush of muleteers, and hawkers, the insults!" She looked up at Maeve with her beautiful black eyes sad. "And the work! Working from before dawn till after dark. I was always so tired, even as a small girl, I never remember having a dream in my whole life."

Maeve smiled at her. "But you work all the time here, Viette."

Viette snapped her fingers in dismissal. "This is nothing! And besides, here I work for myself, and for Bompie, and for our baby. That is very different."

"Yes, that is very different. But since the men are closer to the stockade now, tomorrow let's do a different kind of work. I'll ask Gabriel and Father Daneau to go with us to pick wild cherries. Gabriel tells me there are some black cherry trees nearby."

Viette grinned slyly. "Bompie said Gabriel speaks of you with every breath. He said Gabriel is with you at every chance."

"Oh?" Maeve studied the cradle. "I had not noticed."

When she looked back at Viette, the girl was laughing gaily. Maeve laughed with her.

They picked wild black cherries the next day, and the next, strawberries and raspberries. The men were still wood-cutting, but there was not the haste there had been before and the hunting was excellent. Their foods had great variety—deer, geese, swans, beaver. There seemed to be no end to the meat or fowl or fish, or melon or berry growing wild.

One night as they sat by the fire, Maeve was sewing on a piece of fine English wool. She had dyed it purple with berry juice and was hemming the long, flowing circle.

"That is beautiful," Gabriel said. "What is it?"

"It is a wedding cape. I am getting married when my father returns."

Gabriel's sun-bronzed face paled. He said not a word.

"He is a handsome and dashing man, but what endears him to me the most is that he is heartful."

Still Gabriel said nothing. He looked at her without blinking, his eyes darkening to solid black.

"The only trouble with this man is," and Maeve stared off dreamily into the night, "he has no modesty."

"He . . . he . . . has no modesty?" stammered Gabriel.

"He has no modesty at all!" Maeve said, laughing.

Gabriel jumped up and grabbed both her hands, pulling her to her feet.

"But he is the happiest Frenchman with no modesty in the world!" He whirled her around and around.

When Gabriel announced to the group that he and Maeve were going to be married, he was surprised that no one was surprised.

"I will make you some buttons for the cape," he told Maeve, "from hand-hammered tin." He had made them by the next evening, three big, round buttons of tin with smooth edges but bent facets which caught points of light and gleamed. On the bright purple, they reflected violet-silver. Maeve packed the cape away carefully in the bottom of the trunk to await the return of her father.

Father Daneau taught Maeve about the trees: the rowan tree, the balsam, the tamarack, the red pine, the white ash, the pigeonberry, the maple, and the spruce.

With Gabriel, sometimes with Viette, sometimes joined by Count Rastoff, they walked through the hazy sunlight of the great north woods. If they sat quietly, a fox might appear or a beaver on the river. Once, to Maeve's delight, two little bears, called "cherry bears," clambered up a wild black cherry tree following their mother. To Maeve, it was the most delightful summer of her life.

But the summer was nearing its ending and the travelers had not returned.

Then almost overnight, it was brilliant autumn. Except for the evergreens, every leaf was burnished copper, bronze, and gold. Crimson, too. Radiance filled the hillsides with splendor.

And one of the guards disappeared. The rest of the men set out to search for him and found him by the wild cherry trees—with an arrow through his back. It was a sad burial, and Gabriel was not surprised to find the canoe gone. Three men had deserted in the night.

Maeve and Viette were appalled, but Gabriel said, "One of those men has seven children. The other two are but trying to save their own lives. The wilderness is not for everyone."

And then winter came.

Wind whipped every last gold, bronze, and crimson leaf from the trees and left their black silhouettes against the gray, angry sky. The snow began with dots of white and flew in fury, blotting out everything in a furry white mist. The river water became icy slush as it slowly froze, thick and white along the banks. The tall grass near the water became stalks of ice, brittle and stiff, cracking and splitting in the wind. The first snowstorm lasted three days while the small settlement shivered in crude cabins and hugged the fire, eating dried meat and fish with a bread made of cornmeal and water.

Still Maeve's father, Bompie, and the trappers did not return. Maeve trembled for her father, Bompie, and the others, but she did not talk of it to Viette. The girl was already worried. All their spirits wavered with the eerie wind howling outside and cold seeping through each crack of the cabins.

Huddled around the fire, they kept busy finishing the clothes they had fashioned after the ones Iroquois wore. Maeve had a close-fitting hat of gray squirrel and was finishing gloves of the same fur. Gabriel had his clothes from years before, but his gloves were ragged—and he was poor at sewing. On the third night of the storm, he came to Maeve's cabin covered with snow dust from head to foot, looking like a great white bear bursting in the door with the whirling snow. For Maeve, it was the one bright hour of the tedious day. They sat by the fire sewing, talking in half-French, half-English, and that night with Viette, they drank the last cups of warmed black cherry juice from the cherries they had picked in the summer.

Viette sewed silently while Gabriel struggled with his new gloves, but when he was ready to leave, she rose and reached for Maeve's hand and one of Gabriel's. She knelt and pulled them to their knees.

"We pray," she whispered, "we pray for them. God, He must take care of them."

Maeve squeezed her hand and said, "He will, Viette. I know He will."

"In case He forgets, we remind Him, yes?"

They bowed their heads, the three of them holding hands, and prayed, tears rolling down Viette's plump rosy face and falling on her rounding body.

The next morning when Maeve awoke, there was frost on the ceiling. In spite of her hands and feet feeling almost numb with cold, she thought the sparkling frost was pretty. Dressing hastily, she built up the banked fire. Viette was so far down in her covers that only the top of her curly mop showed. Maeve pulled on layers of clothes to go out for some snow to make soup of dried fish flakes. She knew they must carefully watch their food now. With one arm in her coat, she stopped and listened. The wind had dropped. After the howling of three days, the silence, except for the cracking fire, seemed unnatural. She opened the door and stepped out. The fierce wind had swept clean the ground on the south side of the cabin and piled it to the roof on the other side.

With the sun shining, she saw an enchanted landscape, gleaming bright. The great evergreens were blanketed with snow, and the wind had sculptured snow in mounds and hummocks like waves on the ocean. Awed, Maeve breathed the clear pure air until her lungs ached.

Ice cracked sharply. Count Rastoff, smiling, waved a long

icicle at her from the door of his cabin. His long fur coat must have been tailored in Paris. His otter hat was tied with a silver cord. When he walked toward Maeve, his shining boots crunched the ice. He carried his gun. That surprised her, as he rarely hunted with the other men. Perhaps he felt more comfortable now that the climate was similar to his native Russia. He stood beside her, breathing loudly, his breath visible as smoke.

"Hah! Beautiful, isn't it? Today I will hunt."

"Yes, it is lovely, and some fresh meat will be welcome, welcome." She looked up into his face, his black beard as carefully groomed as if he were at the Russian court. "Does this remind you of home?"

He sighed. "The snow, yes. The rest, no. Oh, if we had a sleigh . . ." but he never finished and walked into the silent snow waves, his footsteps muffled. In a moment, his two men followed with a nod to Maeve. They carried guns as well, and Maeve hoped desperately they were good hunters. She didn't want ever to see a dried fish flake or a dried swan flake again as long as she lived. Nonetheless, she gathered snow and returned to make her soup.

Gabriel had been hunting early and he brought Maeve two squirrels and had bagged four more for the others.

"But we have no more corn for porridge or bread, Gabriel."

Gabriel backed away from the smell of the fish broth and leaned on the wood stacked against the wall. He ran his fingers through his dark hair, now so long it was curling on his shoulders. He sighed. "Then we shall have to trade with that band of Iroquois."

Maeve was startled. "But will they trade with us?"

"Only if we have something they want. We certainly won't trade them guns or ammunition. What do we have?"

"I think Father and Bompie took most everything since we did not intend to trade. That skin in the second room holds all we have left."

When he returned to Maeve from the other room, he had a bundle wrapped in rabbit skin.

"There are very few things. I left a few beads and a kettle. We may need them later." He placed the bundle in his pack. "I'll take Father Daneau. He knows the Iroquois trader named Kimo. That might help."

But Father Daneau thought they should all go in order to show their strength. Even Maeve and Viette carried guns.

Maeve was surprised to see the skin huts of the Iroquois so close to their settlement. Father Daneau and Gabriel approached the four Indians outside their camp. The rest waited under the trees.

There were long pauses when nothing happened at all. Then Maeve saw Father Daneau hold out a kettle to the Iroquois trader. The Indian took it, looked at it and kicked it away into the snow. Again they waited. A figure came from behind one of the skin houses.

It was an old woman. The woman stared at the group under the trees and spit into the snow. She spoke to Father Daneau and he walked back to them. His expression was sheepish.

He said, "The medicine woman, Mishoni, is insulted that we brought squaws to our powwow. Perhaps if you go home, they will trade."

"But . . . but will it be safe to leave you and Gabriel here?"

"They are a small band," Father Daneau said, "and they

know we are armed. Count Rastoff has returned. He and his men will accompany you."

Maeve looked back as they began their walk to the settlement. Gabriel stood military straight, alone with the four Iroquois and the old medicine woman, Mishoni, was watching them leave.

It was a grim afternoon until Gabriel and Father Daneau returned. But they did, and with corn.

When Gabriel handed the bundle to Maeve, she said, shaking her head, "I never want to spend another hour like that!"

Gabriel laughed. "Once you squaws were out of sight, Mishoni, that old medicine woman, was eager to trade for the beads. And Kimo was fairly friendly—for an Iroquois, anyway." He grew more serious. "I think they are not in good shape either. Game has been hard to come by and they looked leaner than the last time I saw them. They would trade eagerly for guns, of course, but it would be deadly to do that."

Christmas and an ice storm arrived on the same day. The distant cliffs were bearded with shining icicles. Hills wrapped in forest glittered from afar. The wood of the hut was covered with transparent ice and Maeve could see the bark of the logs underneath. The roof was fanged with giant icicles two and three feet long. In some places, the huge icicles had been broken loose by the wind and dropped straight down, spearing into the crusted earth. All the cleared meadows made by the men were solid crystal. The trees cracked with their icy weight with a sound like rifle shots.

Maeve admired the spectacular scene, but after a few

minutes, the wind cut through her heaviest clothes as if she wore none. The best Christmas gift would be to see the silhouettes of the travelers against the dazzling white scene for it would be a sad Christmas without them. She kept alive in her heart that though the men could not travel now, in some months the thaw in the spring would bring them back to the settlement. Her deepest fear was that they would never return at all, but she pushed that thought away. She had to appear spirited for the others at Christmas.

Green boughs, fresh smelling, were the only decorations as the whole small settlement—Gabriel, Margarite, Viette, Count Rastoff and his two men, and Father Daneau— crowded into Maeve's cabin for Christmas dinner. Fresh rabbit stew was the main dish and there were a few slabs of beaver Maeve had saved and frozen in anticipation of Gabriel's favorite. Bread was the usual cornmeal and water. Maeve and Viette had tried to vary it by frying in beaver fat, but it was soggy and unsuccessful.

Gifts were few and mostly homemade. Gabriel gave Maeve a handsome inlaid box and she gave him a red squirrel hat. Maeve gave Viette the blue linen jacket she had brought from Britain. Viette's gift to Maeve was her taffeta hood. It was a loving exchange, and everyone had a gift for the baby. Gabriel had polished the cradle until it was as smooth as glass, the black cherry wood gleaming. Margarite had embroidered a tiny white shirt made from her kerchiefs. Father Daneau presented a missal and Count Rastoff, a gold sovereign. Even the two servants of the count had gifts. They had carved wooden toys, a tiny boat and a bird, which they shyly gave to Viette. Maeve had sewed small shoes from white rabbit fur as her gift. Viette accepted the gifts with unnaturally bright eyes and deep gratefulness, but her hands trembled as she placed each gift in the cradle.

The atmosphere grew from quiet to grim as memories of former Christmases returned—Christmases spent with the aroma of roasting fowls, of plum puddings, of honeyed cakes, of sparkling decorations and fine music. Maeve's mother had died after Christmas and Maeve was suddenly so homesick for her family—her father, her jolly aunt, and her younger sisters—that she could hardly hold back her tears. Count Rastoff stared morosely into the fire and Margarite appeared to be lost in prayer.

All at once Viette burst into loud weeping. Maeve put her arm around the girl's shaking shoulders and said, "I understand, Viette. We all miss those from home."

But Viette looked up with brimming eyes. "Not me! I don't miss home. This is the best Christmas I ever had ... except for Bompie being gone. He's never coming back! He's never coming back!" And she cried afresh.

Gabriel wedged himself on the other side of Viette and whispered in French. After a few minutes, he dried Viette's tears until she was only sobbing quietly. He continued to whisper, and Maeve could hear the word "Bompie" in almost every sentence. At last, he said something which coaxed a little smile to Viette's lips. Then he began to sing a French song. It was a lively tune and, in a quavering voice, Viette joined him. Soon Margarite was singing, her clear voice rising above the others. Father Daneau sang, too, though his strong tones were off-key. Gabriel set the tempo faster and faster until they were breathless to keep up. And laughing.

Maeve was thinking how good it was to hear Viette laughing again when Count Rastoff suddenly rose. Have we offended him? she wondered. His men rose also, but he motioned them to stay and he left the cabin.

Out of loyalty to her own, Maeve began to sing an old English lullaby and was surprised when Margarite, her usually sad eyes brightening, sang with her—in French. They smiled to each other at the garbled duet, but the tone kept the festive mood alive. Count Rastoff returned with a bottle half full of brandy. With such a crowd, it was only a teaspoonful in each cup of hot water, but it was his sharing that endeared him. Not to be outdone by the French, he commanded his two men to their feet and they sang a lusty Russian soldier's song at the top of their voices. It was a startling rendition, and revealed the count's fierce pride in his country.

But the French had greater numbers. They set about teaching Maeve, the count and his two men the song they had originally sung. With much laughing and repetition, they finally managed a slow version. It was after midnight when the rest of the group, now closer in spirit, shouted, "Good night, Merry Christmas," and crunched across the ice-glazed ground to their cold, dark cabins.

By the middle of February, Gabriel and Father Daneau made their last journey to the band of Iroquois to trade for corn. It was their last journey because they had nothing else to trade. The Algonquins might have *given* them corn, but the Iroquois, *never*. Gabriel brought back bad news as well. The Indians were sickening. Kimo, who had traded with them before, and several others, had swollen knee joints as big as small trees.

"And while I bartered with him, Kimo, I noticed his teeth were loose, Maeve." He wrinkled his nose. "And he smelled."

Maeve threw him a glance, smiling. "I have noticed they often smell, Gabriel."

Gabriel shook his head. "Not like that. This was not from lack of bathing. It was something else."

"What about Mishoni, the medicine woman? Was she with them?"

"I did not see Mishoni, but Father Daneau is afraid the sickness will spread to us." His gaze was serious. "We cannot defend ourselves if we are weak."

Together, they watched Viette and Margarite grinding the corn for bread.

"For all of us," Maeve said, "this corn will only last three days. We had better have lots of good hunting," and she gave Gabriel a mischievous glance, "because all we have left is dried fish flakes."

"Ugh!" groaned Gabriel. "Tomorrow, Father Daneau and I will hunt. Count Rastoff and his men should go, too. We can at least have fresh meat."

But Gabriel did not hunt the next day. A snow squall blotted out the sky with white flurries. Another ice storm followed. Then a blizzard. The river was frozen across, solid and hard.

And Father Daneau sickened. His knees began to swell and his teeth ached. Gabriel rubbed turpentine on the priest's limbs, but after it raised blisters on Father Daneau's skin, he stopped. Margarite took care of Father Daneau, but his knees swelled bigger and bigger and his teeth became so loose he could not have chewed meat—if they had any.

Then Gabriel sickened.

And Margarite.

And Vashi, one of Count Rastoff's men.

Maeve moved all the sick ones into the middle cabin and she cared for them there. She slept in her own cabin at night and kept Viette away from the sick. She was fearful Viette, whose baby was due soon, would catch the sickness.

Maeve pondered what she could do for the sick, except in their weakness, give them water, fish broth, and keep the fire going. Gabriel was the most cheerful one, and Maeve felt he kept up the show for her. Sometimes, she had nothing to say, and sat by his bed holding his hands cradled in her own.

But there was the smell.

In the small room with the fire constantly going, their teeth reeked. Maeve would stay as long as she could bear it, then hasten outside to the bitingly cold air—and retch.

On one such hour, she glimpsed three Iroquois loitering quite close in the meadow. Her heart thundered. Did they know how weak and sick the settlers were?

She dashed into her own cabin where Viette was stirring fish soup.

"Viette," she cried, "grab two pieces of firewood and beat on the walls."

"*What?*" Viette was astonished.

"Do it *now!*" and Maeve ran to the third cabin where a surprised Count Rastoff looked up from his reading.

"Please beat on the walls—you and your man—so that the band of Iroquois will think we are all working!"

As she left, the count was rising.

At her command, the sick ones dragged themselves to the

cabin walls and hammered with firewood. All except Father Daneau. He was too weak to move. Gabriel and the others could not continue for long, but they rested and began again at intervals. It gave the sound of life and activity for most of the day. When Maeve again went out, the Indians were gone.

The next day Count Rastoff, dressed for travel, came to Maeve's cabin. He told her they must leave.

She stared at him blankly. *"Leave?"*

"Back to Quebec. You and I and my man, we must try."

She glanced at Viette, who was covered by furs, taking a nap.

Her voice was low. "I cannot leave. The others are too weak to take care of themselves. They need water and food and the fire kept up. And there's Viette and the baby."

Count Rastoff stared into the fire for a long moment.

Then he spoke. "They will die. They will all die."

Maeve's voice was a mere whisper. "I would stay to help the others, but I love Gabriel. I would never abandon him."

"You are young. You will find another. Come."

Maeve shook her head. "No."

The count turned away from her sadly, his hand on the door.

"Wait," Maeve said, "I will walk to the edge of the stockade with you." She pulled on her rabbit coat and snugged her cap over her ears.

Outside, the air was crisp, and though all was frozen, the snow, untrod, was pure and clean.

Maeve said, "I wish you good fortune, Count, but I do not believe you will survive the long journey back to Quebec.

You will be two men alone. That is dangerous with roving bands of Iroquois."

The count gave her a slow, sad smile. "You are probably correct." And he gestured toward the beauty before him. "But I would rather die in this clean snow than in a stinking hole. I have watched you every day leave the sickroom and retch."

Maeve had no answer. She shook his hand and turned back as his man came from the cabin carrying a large pack. He nodded to Maeve and joined the count. Maeve was certain they would not survive.

Maeve walked slowly back to the sickroom. She bathed Margarite's face and gave Father Daneau a drink of water. Vashi, the count's man, never asked for anything, but he murmured thanks for everything she did. When she approached Gabriel, he did not open his eyes or respond. When she held his hand, it was limp. He was breathing, but barely. Maeve was so overcome that she left the cabin and stumbled out into the snow. Outside the stockade she struggled through the banks to the low hanging limb of a balsam tree. She sat down on it, covered her face with her hands, and cried as if her heart would break.

Without a sound, a sudden weight joined her on the limb and it shook. Maeve leaped up, scattering snow, terrified. A Great Snowy Owl was sitting on the limb, its enormous eyes turned on her.

"Look about you," the owl said.

Maeve did nothing but stare at the owl, and it repeated. "Look about you."

Maeve did because she saw Indians out of the corner of

her eye. It was three Iroquois, one of them Kimo. If Maeve was surprised to hear an owl talking to her, she was just as amazed to see Kimo healed, strong and healthy, walking on the frozen river.

"Mishoni," the owl said before Maeve could gather her wits. "Speak with Mishoni, the medicine woman."

I must be having visions, Maeve thought, rubbing her eyes. Her teeth were chattering and she thought her blood must be congealing from the cold. When she looked at the limb again, the great white owl glared at her with huge green eyes.

"Mishoni."

Suddenly Maeve blurted, "I cannot go to Mishoni alone! She will not talk to me. She is a medicine woman and I am just a squaw!"

"Do you want Gabriel to live?"

Maeve's eyes opened wide. *"Oh, yes!"*

"I will go with you. Wear your purple wool cape."

"My wedding cape ..." Maeve stopped speaking at the fierce gaze of the owl.

"You must bring something to trade. Make haste."

Still not sure she was not losing her wits, Maeve ran back to the stockade. First she fairly flew to Gabriel's side.

"Gabriel, Gabriel," she whispered, her mouth close to his ear. "Can you hear me?"

He shook his head, but did not open his eyes.

"Gabriel, I saw Kimo. He was *well!*" She stopped for breath. "And, Gabriel, a Great Snowy Owl told me to talk to Mishoni, the medicine woman."

At this, Gabriel opened his eyes and looked at her. His

voice was so weak Maeve had to put her ear close to hear. "My love, you are exhausted. Your mind is wandering. Go lie by the fire and rest!" Then his head fell back and he closed his eyes again.

But Maeve unfolded her wedding cape and then rummaged for something to trade. She could think of nothing they had not already traded which would appeal to the medicine woman. Beads, kettles, hatchets—all those things had been traded.

My silver medallion.

That is all I have.

She reached into the bottom of her trunk and picked up the soft cloth the medallion was wrapped in. Then she buttoned on her long flowing cape and hurried back to the owl.

The owl, with silent wings—no whirring at all—landed on Maeve's shoulders with a white feathery foot on each side of her neck.

We are probably an impressive sight, thought Maeve, but I fear we have not much protection from a band of Indians.

"How shall I find Mishoni?" asked Maeve.

"Follow the river."

Out on the smooth ice, Maeve walked. It was far easier than trying to traverse the snow. In the great silence, she heard the boom of an avalanche. In the distance, white plumes flew high into the sky. Otherwise everything was still.

Maeve walked on the river until she saw smoke from a fire, then bright flames on the bank and there was the old medicine woman, Mishoni.

"No matter what she does, do not move. Stay perfectly

still," said the owl in a low voice. Maeve walked straight and dignified, though her knees shook, to the woman's fire.

If Mishoni was surprised or alarmed to see a redheaded woman in a long purple cape, a Great Snowy Owl on her shoulders, she gave no sign. She stirred the pot she had on her fire, and fumbled with branches of spruce lying on the snow. Maeve stayed perfectly still until the woman gave her her attention.

Seeing the hostile eyes in the wrinkled face, Maeve suddenly panicked. It would be extremely dangerous to let this Iroquois know that the men on the settlement were sick, that there were only two women there, one of them heavy with child.

She stared into the old leathery face, hoping desperately that the fierce green eyes of the owl were staring, too. Calmly, she said, "I am the French medicine woman. I fly with the Great Snowy Owl."

The medicine woman's eyes widened slightly, but she said nothing. Maeve prepared to wait. Having watched Gabriel trading with the Iroquois, she knew there were long pauses. She waited. And waited.

When it seemed that her feet had become blocks of ice, Maeve said, "We bring a gift to warm by the fire of the powerful medicine woman, Mishoni."

She unrolled the medallion from its cloth, and much as she hated to part with her family heirloom, without looking she handed it to the medicine woman.

Mishoni turned the scrollwork over in her hand. Maeve looked at it then. The medallion was black with tarnish. The silver had no shine at all.

Mishoni dropped it at her feet and then kicked it out into the snow, the ultimate rejection of a gift.

Her knife flashed as she moved toward Maeve. Maeve's impulse was to break and run as fast as her trembly legs could carry her, but the owl's talons tightened into needles on her shoulders. Maeve stood her ground.

The knife flicked across Maeve's chest and a bright tin button fell into Mishoni's hand. Then another and another with a movement almost too swift to see. Maeve began to breathe normally again as her cape loosened and only the owl's feet held it on her shoulders.

In a guttural voice, the medicine woman spoke. "You and your owl may warm at the fire of Mishoni."

The snow had melted in the pot and Maeve watched anxiously to see what the woman placed in it. She was sure she was close to the answer to the sickness. But Mishoni put nothing in it. She continued to cut spruce branches and twigs and stack them at her feet. Then, with her knife, Mishoni scraped the bark from the branches of spruce. Maeve kept casting her eyes around to see what she possibly meant to boil but she could find nothing.

Just when her disappointment was at its height, Mishoni picked up a handful of spruce needles, crushed them, and as the water began to bubble, she dropped handfuls of the spruce needles and scraped bark into the water. She continued to fill the pot in this way until the decoction was boiling rapidly and gave off a slightly skunky smell. Maeve kept waiting to see what else she would throw in the pot, but the medicine woman added nothing.

When Maeve thought she had watched the pot boil for

an hour, she said, "Mishoni is a powerful medicine woman. It is good to warm by her fire."

Mishoni made no sign that she heard and Maeve picked up her medallion with one swoop and then walked as fast as possible on stiff legs to the river.

She was unaware, in her mad rush to get to the stockade, just when the Snowy Owl left. It was only later when her shoulders felt lighter that she knew the bird had lifted into its silent flight.

Maeve put snow in the pot to boil and within an hour and a half, she had made the decoction she had watched the medicine woman make. As soon as it cooled enough to swallow, she took it to the sickroom. Gabriel shook his head when she tried to get him to drink it.

"No," he complained. "It smells skunky, worse than fish." He dropped his head back on his bed. Maeve held his nose, opened his mouth and poured it in. He sputtered and glared, but she had already moved to Margarite, who silently drank it, then Father Daneau and the little Russian, Vashi. "Thank you," Vashi said, but Maeve was hurrying back to her own cabin where she woke Viette and made her drink it, too. Viette was not sick, but Maeve thought perhaps she would not catch the sickness if she drank it. Then holding her own nose—it *did* smell skunky—she drank some herself. She had no idea how much the sick should have, but she dosed them with a swallow or two every hour she was awake.

She had other dreads: Margarite was too sick to deliver Viette's baby and Maeve was terrified she herself would be faced with helping with the birth. She had not the experience to do it. Also, she knew Viette was getting weaker and weaker

81

from lack of food. Oh, how Maeve wished she had learned to hunt. Gabriel had offered to teach her once and she had declined. How foolish! If they survived, she determined she would learn to hunt. It was a necessity to know in this untamed country.

The next morning she was again pouring the medicine into the sick. Gabriel was the only stubborn one. She didn't hesitate to hold his nose and pour it down him. He had to be forced to drink his fish broth as well, but she knew he would not survive without nourishment and there was nothing else. Viette was sleeping too much and Maeve insisted she walk around and around the cabin. The girl had dark circles under her eyes and her arms looked like bones, but she was cooperative; Maeve grieved because Viette did not laugh anymore.

The fourth morning, Father Daneau and Gabriel were sitting up when Maeve entered the sickroom. She didn't have to fight Gabriel to get Mishoni's medicine down. He clasped her hands and held them imprisoned in his own. His eyes told her all she could ever want to know. Vashi, the little Russian, grabbed her hand and kissed it. "I am your servant," he said. "I owe you my life. Now I give you mine."

"Oh, no, Vashi. I am very happy you are getting well, but you owe me nothing."

But from that moment, as soon as he could, Vashi was her servant—hunting, washing, building the fires, whatever needed to be done, he did it.

Margarite was the slowest to get well, but at last she was sitting up and asking for Father Daneau to hear her confession.

At the end of the week, Gabriel, Father Daneau, and

Vashi, though they were far from strong, took their guns and sat at the edge of the stockade. The only game they bagged was rabbit, but never was a hare so heavenly in a stew. When Maeve told them that the medicine was only spruce, crushed leaves and bark, they almost stripped the lower parts of the tree, making the decoction. In two weeks, their swelling had gone, their teeth were no longer loose, and they were regaining their strength with the fresh meat they shot.

In April, the thaw came. The river was violent in its turbulence when the travelers returned. They had been captured by Iroquois and rescued by Algonquins. Maeve's father told her they had been stricken, as had the Indians, by a terrible sickness. The medicine man had healed them with some strange drink. And Father Jean had stayed with the tribe.

"We had the sickness, too, Father." She told him about Mishoni, but hesitated to mention the Great Snowy Owl. Now she wondered if that really did happen or if, in her worry, she had only imagined it. Gabriel was convinced she had a wandering mind that day. She kept that story to herself.

Three days after Bompie, Maeve's father, and the trappers returned, Viette gave birth to the first baby of the settlement. Bompie proudly named his little son Zacherie Cartier Champlain, but called him Zack.

On the evening of that same day, Maeve, wearing her purple cape fastened at the neck by a very shiny silver medallion, was married to Gabriel de Chombray. The place they chose for the ceremony, officiated by Father Daneau, was outside the stockade under a ragged spruce tree.

4.
Maeve Nicole − 2000

It is not only fine feathers that make fine birds.

Aesop, *Fables*

Wherein Maeve's family has moved down the eastern coast of North America to New York City. They are now citizens of the United States. Maeve Nicole is finishing an internship in veterinary medicine. The Scathach arrives in New York City, too.

Maeve Nicole panted as she turned the corner on Cocteau Avenue. The bus had thrown a beige spume as it pulled away from the curb, making her cough. She accelerated again, her running shoes slipping on a discarded plastic wrapper lying on the sidewalk. She heard the loud strains of "Venus and Mars, Star Wars or Candy Bars," the most popular song of the year. Somebody's boom box was drowning the buzzes, roars, and purrs of the cars jockeying for position in the evening rush. Her backpack swung to the left as she swerved past two men carrying lunch pails. One pail banged into her knee. She was tempted to yell, "Watch it!" but she needed the breath for the run. Her lungs were aching now and she was glad she could see the acrylic dome of the University Animal Hospital. She jogged in place waiting for a red light, telling herself she would soon be in the shower at the animal hospital.

She was in the middle of the street when the roar bore down on her; rising above the other noise, it was earsplitting, overpowering and was upon her before she really broke her concentration: a motorcycle, a huge black monster of a motorcycle which wasn't stopping for the light—or pedestrians either.

Maeve Nicole stopped, paralyzed with indecision as to whether to go forward or backward. The cycle passed so close that she fell, catapulted by the rush of air.

Dazed, she felt hands on her arms, and a murmur of voices. Her vision blurred, but she knew she was being led. Her feet were making steps.

Her vision cleared. The murmurs became words.

"Are you all right?"

"Young hoodlum ran right through the light!"

"Ought to be locked up."

"Can you walk?"

Strands of her red hair hung in front of Maeve Nicole's eyes. She couldn't see her benefactors. She brushed her hair away. A young black man in a gray suit, white shirt and navy blue tie was holding her left arm. He said, "Did you break anything?"

Maeve only felt shaken now, except the palm of her right

hand stung. She gave the man a shaky smile. "I—I think I'm okay now. Thanks. Shook me up mostly."

She started to turn the palm of her right hand to look at it and realized others still held onto her arm. A bearded blond man in a running suit similar to her own was frowning at her hand.

"You scraped your hand," he said. "Do you have a handkerchief?"

An older man standing in front of her—she hadn't noticed him—said, "Here. I have one," and he wrapped it around the bloody hand.

"Can you stand okay?"

"Yes, I think so." The hands released her. She moved her shoulders and stretched her legs. Everything seemed to be in working order. Suddenly a blue-jacketed arm slid between the men and a hand with long scarlet nails pushed a necklace, the chain broken and dangling, into Maeve's hands. It was a silver medallion cased in a circle of acrylic. The woman said, "You dropped this when you fell."

Maeve said, "Oh, thanks, *thanks*. It was my great-great-grand . . ."

"S'okay." And the woman withdrew quickly. "Gotta get the kids from the sitter."

Maeve spoke to the group. "Listen, I really thank you, all of you. Who are those people who say New Yorkers don't care? Thank you."

The running-suiter asked again, "Sure you're okay?"

A rumbling bus pulled up to the curb and she spoke over the noise. "I'm fine."

The other two men waved and climbed on the bus.

89

As the bus pulled away, Maeve unwrapped the handker-chief and looked at her palm. It stung, but she was lucky. She could have had an injury much more serious than a scraped hand.

Hand! Maeve was startled out of her reverie—almost out of her wits.

A *hand*—a small gnarled human hand was hanging from under the lid of a garbage can. As Maeve watched, transfixed, the fingers of the bony hand curved and flexed. Then slowly, the forefinger beckoned. Almost undone with amazement, Maeve inched forward. The lid was askew on the garbage can to allow the hand, which she now observed was con-nected to a wrist and then to an arm. Gingerly, Maeve lifted the lid a bit more.

Like a small explosion, a little pug-faced old woman screeched at her. "Well, get me out of here. Don't stand there gaping." She banged on the rim of the garbage can with her hand. "Close your mouth, looks like a cave hanging open like that, *get me out of here!*" She rose half out of the can, brushing a red paper napkin from her arm, then grabbed a blackened banana peel curled on her shoulder and threw it viciously to the sidewalk.

Maeve's surprise was still overwhelming, but she held out both her hands to the old woman and leaned heavily on the garbage can so that it would not tip. The old woman, crouching timorously, stepped on the rim, grasped Maeve in a stranglehold around the throat, closing her windpipe. Si-multaneously the little woman leaped from the rim of the garbage can, swinging her leather-sandaled feet in an arc, which ended on Maeve's shin, right on that sensitive spot where the flesh and skin barely cover the bone. Maeve, struggling for air, bent forward in pain—and the woman's feet hit the sidewalk. Maeve's hands were already pulling the arms from around her neck, but they snapped away.

The outrageous creature was brushing the crumbs and debris from the fur vest she was wearing. For the moment, Maeve's attention was on her own aching shin. She rubbed it to ease the pain. Finally she stood upright and peered down at the woman, who hardly came to her shoulder.

Almost catlike, the bag lady was cleaning the mangy-looking fur, brushing it, rubbing spots, spitting on her hand and diligently working over bits of melted sticky ice cream and a deep red spot of wine on the hem. The vest struck the short woman just above the knee. Under that she wore a dress of some dingy color of brown. Her nose was short and looked pushed back on her face, almost flat, and her alert otter-eyes stared out of folded flesh and a mass of wrinkles. Her hair was short and kinky, pepper-and-salt. Her skin, to Maeve's eye, looked as if it had weathered many snowstorms, a few burning desert winds, and at least eighty-nine summers of hard bright sunshine. Her legs were covered with coarse wool stockings, and toes stuck out of the leather sandals. She was the strangest bag lady Maeve Nicole had ever seen.

As Maeve finished this study, the old woman looked up at her with eyes like brown pebbles.

Maeve, straightening the pack on her back, said, "I know it's none of my business and I'm about to be late for work anyway, but—I can't help asking, why were you in the garbage can?"

"Protecting myself."

"Protecting yourself?"

"Yes, from that black snorting monster, that whirly, whirly . . ." She spun her gnarled hands around like wheels.

"Oh, the motorcycle! Good Lord, yes! You were wise— he almost hit me and I fell—" She showed the woman her bandaged hand. "Well, I guess we're both okay. I've got to get to work." She smiled. "Good-bye."

The small woman grabbed her arm. "Wait, you can't go till you get my bag."

"What bag?"

"In there." She pointed a crooked finger at the garbage can.

Maeve sighed, walked over and peered in the can. She saw a leathery-looking travelling bag. She was thunderstruck because the bag was of fine quality. When she lifted it out, it was heavy.

"Ugh!" She set it on the sidewalk. "How can you carry that? And how beautiful!" The travelling bag was of some unusual reptile skin, looked very old, but was smooth and intact. "Is this alligator?"

"Sea serpent," the woman replied, grasping the handle of the bag.

Maeve looked startled, then laughed. "I'll bet there aren't many of those around."

The pudgy wrinkled face broke into a smile, and she chuckled. "Right. It's the only one in the world." She thrust the braided skin handles of the travelling bag at Maeve. "As long as you're going that way, could you carry it for me?"

"Oh, might as well, but I'm just going to the animal hospital there at the end of the next block."

They started off together, walking briskly.

The woman said, "You going to work, you say? It's almost night."

"I'm a veterinarian, and I'm 'on call' tonight," Maeve answered.

"A what?"

"I'm an animal doctor. I'm finishing my internship this week and I have a job interview tomorrow."

Maeve dodged around a woman carrying a baby and swung the heavy bag to her other hand.

The curved acrylic door of the animal hospital was colored to look like a rainbow.

The clear acrylic wall beside the arched-rainbow door was splattered with spray paint, a smudged combination of black and orange. A man was cleaning it.

"Oh, no, not again!" said Maeve.

When she spoke, the young man who was diligently scrubbing the splattered wall looked at her. He said, "Yes, the Whips and Flames are having their graffiti war again—leaving their tag on everything." He stooped and dipped his scrub brush in a bucket of chemical at his feet. He kicked at the pile of soiled rags on the sidewalk. "Sam and I have been cleaning this up all day." He whooshed out his breath. "They'll move off to another part of the city now."

"I certainly hope so—but what makes you think so?" Maeve asked.

The workman grinned. "This place is swarming with cops, that's why! And the Whips and the Flames are at the top of their list."

Maeve frowned. "The Whips are bad enough, lashing and cracking those long black evil snaky things—" She turned to the old woman and shook her head. "But the Flames, they're the worst, so destructive, so dangerous." She set the bag down at the woman's feet. "I have to go to work now, but do you know about New York City's program for bag ladies? The ground floors of some of our office buildings are open so you can sleep there. It's not great, but it's safe with the security guards. I can give you a list of the buildings."

The old woman drew her small body up in a gesture of hauteur. Her pebbly eyes glittered with scorn.

"*I* am no bag lady! I am *touring!*"

Maeve was abashed, but skeptical. "I'm sorry. I didn't mean to insult you, and I do have to go now. Enjoy your tour." She walked into the glossy hall and toward the receptionist to check in.

Inside the waiting room, most of the acrylic benches were empty as fewer accidents take place at night when people have their pets at home with them watching television. But there were always sick animals. A Manx cat set up an eerie howl when Maeve walked in, and a big white Lab growled, tugging on the leash held by a young girl. Two other cats lounged in carrying cases with their masters and a fragile old man rested a monkey cage beside him. The see-through benches, new like the rest of the hospital, were easy to clean, but were already scarred from numerous protesting paws and claws.

Perhaps it will be a quiet night, Maeve thought, and in the next moment, found the small old woman at her heels.

Maeve said, "Hey, this is a hospital, and you can't wander around in it."

"You don't let tourists visit? You don't show tourists around?" the woman countered.

"Yes, we do, but you have to have a pass. You have to get that from the receptionist. What's your name?"

Temporarily flustered, the old woman hesitated. She scanned the room with her eyes, then looked through the clear acrylic walls to a big sign advertising Saks Fifth Avenue.

"Saks," she said.

Maeve looked at her skeptically. "Your name is *Saks*? Saks *what*? The receptionist will have to write your full name on your pass."

With defiance, the woman stared at Maeve. "Saks Fifth Avenue."

They were nearing the receptionist's black lacquered desk and Maeve, laughing, began, "You can't . . ."

The old woman interrupted her with a laser-beam stare.

"Okay," Maeve said, shaking her head. "We'll just say your name is Saks."

Maeve suddenly stopped.

"Uh-oh, we have a temp."

"A temp?" the old woman asked.

"A temporary receptionist instead of our regular," Maeve whispered. "This one, Dawn, has worked here before but she never seems to remember our routine."

The temporary receptionist looked up with a smile on her brightly painted lips. She was briskly polishing the already gleaming black desk. Not a scrap of paper was on it. Only a brilliant red telephone with enough buttons and dials to fly an airplane.

"Hello, Dawn," Maeve said. "We need a visitor's pass for this lady."

Dawn bent her curly turquoise-haired head; her drop earrings, the size of robin's eggs, bobbed and bounced on her slender neck. She scrabbled in the first drawer on her desk, then the second, and pulled out the third with an impatient yank.

"What color is it?" the receptionist asked with a puzzled frown.

"It's bright yellow," Maeve sighed. "Haven't we had any visitors today?"

"Well, yes," the girl pouted, pulling the yellow blanks from her first drawer, "but there's a lot to remember around here and I forgot. Gee."

"It's all right, Dawn. Tell you what," Maeve answered, "I'll just fill in the blanks for you. I'm in kind of a hurry."

She filled in the blanks quickly and took Saks by the arm, hurrying toward the elevator.

"Hey," called Dawn. "Her name is *Saks*? Saks what?"

But Maeve pretended not to hear and, as the elevator came, they stepped in. As the door slid closed, Maeve saw Dawn vigorously wiping her desk to remove any fingerprints.

Through the glass sides of the elevator, they watched silently as lights of the metropolis began to twinkle ruby, diamond, sapphire, and emerald in the dusky violet of twilight. Streaks of vivid neon slashed across the face of buildings, the fumes of traffic fusing them with halos and misty auras, a spectacular light show. The great city of New York glittered, a giant draped in rhinestones.

When they left the elevator, Maeve seated Saks in the interns' dressing room while she cleaned her scraped hand with antiseptic, then showered. She stuffed her running clothes and Saks's bag in her locker and hung up the blue linen suit she had brought for her job interview.

Saks was asleep in a big brown corduroy chair when Maeve returned in her pale green shirt, jacket, and matching pants, her working clothes.

"I only have about twenty minutes and this is a big hospital, but I'll show you what I can." Maeve Nicole waited while a sleepy Saks stood up and yawned. Then she continued, "Volunteers show visitors around during the day, but we don't have any on the night shift."

In the Intensive Care Unit, the walls were lined with large and small cages. The radio was softly playing, "Venus and Mars, Star Wars or Candy Bars." Maeve wondered if the animals liked it as much as everyone else seemed to. Four cats, all Persian, a cocker spaniel, a pit bull, and a miniature goat were in the ICU. One cat meowed, a dog whimpered, and the goat appeared to be asleep.

"The goat had surgery today because he swallowed a piece of string that had to be removed."

In an adjoining room, a handsome Irish setter and a German shepherd barked excitedly and strained at their leashes when Maeve spoke to them and stroked their heads.

"These boys are ready to go home tomorrow. That German shepherd guard dog had a gunshot wound from a burglar." She commanded the German shepherd to "sit" and he obeyed immediately. The Irish setter continued to bark, jump to the end of his leash, wiggling his slender body in joy at the attention. "Sit, Cuchulain! I can't hear myself think!" Maeve said, but the dog continued its frenzied jumping and yapping.

"Sit!" commanded Saks. The setter stopped in midleap, licked his mouth twice and, silent, set his rump on the floor.

97

"Well!" Maeve said, surprised. "You sure have command with animals. What I was going to say above Cuchulain's noise is that the gorgeous creature is one of my favorite dogs. But he's here too often because he's undisciplined. This time he ate his mistress's heart medicine. She can't seem to understand that it's not a kindness to let her pet run wild."

When she closed the door behind her, both dogs were sitting quietly.

They walked on through the corridor and Maeve pointed out the operating room. "That's the operating room, but we can't go in as it has to be kept sterile."

A group of people came through the swinging doors at the end of the hall.

Maeve said, "Oops. That's evening rounds. Those two women in white are teaching doctors and the others are interns. I have to join that group." She reached in a closet and pulled out a folding chair. "You sit here and wait, Saks, but you will be able to see us through the glass. We'll be talking about each patient and its treatment. Okay?"

Saks sat down without a word and Maeve rushed to join the others who were going into the ICU.

Saks was asleep, scrunched in the corner half under the folding chair when Maeve shook her gently.

"We've had a call from the Animal Health Center at the zoo and I have to go there to assist Dr. Wallen. You can find your way out, can't you? I hope you liked your tour. Good luck."

Saks uncurled herself and stretched.

"What's happening at the zoo?"

Maeve was walking toward the elevator and she spoke over her shoulder. "A tiger, Emperor Ben, swallowed a basketball and we have to remove it." She pushed the button for the elevator as two of the interns ambled by, both of them looking out of the corners of their eyes at Saks.

"Tiger swallowed a basketball?" Saks frowned darkly at Maeve as if she didn't believe her.

"But, Saks, he really did. Some vandal bounced it into the tiger habitat, and like a humongous kitten—because the ball was moving—Emperor Ben pounced on it, his teeth deflated it, and he chewed it up and swallowed it."

"How are you going to get it out?" Saks asked.

"Very carefully!" Then, more serious, Maeve said, "Dr. Wallen will remove it. I'm only going to assist." She waved at Saks as the elevator door closed.

On the fifth floor, Maeve worked the combination on a metal safe and opened the door. From the shelf inside, she lifted one of the three personal rockets. She locked the safe again and then fitted on the parachutelike straps with the rocket pack on her back. The Air Force had loaned the rockets to the veterinarians for observing the zoo animals in their extensive native habitats and for emergencies, but their use was highly restricted. There were only ten in use in the country outside the military. Though Maeve's trip was not strictly an emergency, the straight route on the rocket was a lot faster than the circuitous trip by car.

Maeve unlocked the door to the outside, settled on the small landing pad, gave the jets a few minutes to warm and then chugged, puffing white smoke behind her, toward the zoo. The rocket was not really powerful and she felt only a slight breeze from the slow speed. She flew at low altitude, but the pedestrians on the sidewalk did not often look up and she saw no one below gaping.

Saks, who had taken the next elevator, watched Maeve depart, then walked to the locked metal safe. She didn't touch it, but fixed the lock with an emerald green laser-beam stare. The door flew open. She strapped on the rocket as she had seen Maeve do, and turned it on, squinching her nose at the jet fuel fumes. Scornful of the smelly puffing mechanism strapped on her back, she switched the rocket off.

She then grew her own wings, transparent violet, the color of dusk, freckled with the sparkling colors of the city lights. With this camouflage, she sailed out over the New York streets toward the zoo.

The session with the tiger in the Animal Health Center was long and tedious, but went smoothly. The enormous beast was stretched out to his full length on a long metal table; his huge paws dwarfed Maeve's small hands. His pumpkin orange fur, with its inky black stripes was magnificent. Maeve ran her hand over his rich coat, shuddering at the thought that most of his cousins had died so humans could use their fur. Emperor Ben was a rare, priceless animal.

But his teeth! His mouth was propped open with cushioned acrylic sticks for Dr. Wallen to work through the tube down his throat. Those huge molars and fangs glistened white and sharp. As a carnivore, he needed them to tear meat, but Maeve was grateful he was anesthetized. In his heart, he was wild, a creature never to be really tame, though he was not always dangerous to humans. He knew Maeve and often, when he saw her, gave her a *prusten*—a tiger's greeting of blowing through his lips.

Because Maeve was only assisting Dr. Wallen, her job was not difficult; it consisted of occasional checks of blood pressure and handling the instruments. The hospital and the zoo had the most sophisticated machines in the world—scanners, artificial lungs, and monitors, but the interns had to be trained to use their hands, eyes, and ears in the event they had jobs where the equipment was primitive.

Maeve watched fascinated as Dr. Wallen, through the tube, pulled out tiny pieces of the basketball Emperor Ben had swallowed. The tiger also had a tube down his nose to be sure he had oxygen and his great rasping breath could be heard around the room.

Saks huddled in a dim corner, unnoticed by the interns, doctor, and zoo personnel gathered under the bright lights.

When the work was finished, and Emperor Ben lay sleeping, two of the other interns were assigned to the tiger's care and Maeve was ready to leave. It was then that she saw Saks lurking in the corner. Frowning, Maeve hissed in a whisper, "Sneak out that door as fast as you can—you're going to get me in *big* trouble."

Hurriedly, Maeve called, "Good night," to the chatting group, and dashed through the door, pushed Saks around the corner of the building, and stopped for breath. "Take that rocket off! For Pete's sake, you have to have a permit and a license and practically have the president to vouch for your character before you can use one of these rockets!

They aren't even *ours*. They belong to the Air Force." Maeve began undoing the parachutelike straps from Saks's body. "Now we're going to take the *bus* back to the hospital, even if it rains." Maeve looked up at the low-hanging clouds that had replaced the stars. "How did you work the combination on the safe, anyway?"

Saks blinked her little round eyes innocently and looked up at the sky. "It's sprinkling already. Do you have an umbrella?"

"Yes, but it's at the hospital."

Maeve stretched her arms over her head. The fresh air was welcome after hours spent enclosed with the odor of bodies, both human and animal, overlaid with antiseptic and medicinal smells. She breathed deeply and Saks sniffed beside her.

Maeve reached down, touching her toes three times to relieve the stiffness. "Okay. Let's head for the gate and catch a bus." She yawned and watched Saks rub her eyes with a fist like a small child.

They walked through the murky night, cutting across paths to reach the main gate where the bus stopped. A bus was already there.

The gate had to be opened with an electronic card, and, in spite of Maeve's yells, the bus pulled away as they hurried through. "Oh, well," she said, "there's another bus stop a couple of blocks from here with a more direct route to the hospital anyway." She took Saks's arm. "It's just that four o'clock in the morning is not an ideal time to be wandering around the city."

The small shops were closed tightly, grills covering their

102

display windows, dim night-lights glowing in their depths. Shadows and dark shapes of nothing lurked in the doorways and alleys. Auras of amber surrounded the streetlamps like halos and the pavement began to glisten as fine soft rain fell. A night bird shrieked at the zoo. The only other sound was the *squish* of Maeve's rubber-soled oxfords and the shuffle of Saks's sandals. Hush had fallen as if the giant city of New York had gone to sleep, covered with a dark blanket smothering sound.

As they reached the second block, Maeve stopped, tilting her head to listen.

"Wait," she said. "What's that shouting?" She looked into Saks's upturned pudgy face. "Do you hear it?"

Saks pointed a gnarled finger toward the connecting street. Maeve heard the shouts, then a sharp *crack!*

Feet were pounding, pelting the sidewalk—many running feet—and sharp sounds *crackled.*

"The Whips!" Maeve said. "A gang war!" She grabbed Saks's arm and pulled her, the little woman stumbling and panting to keep up. Maeve dashed back to the telephone kiosk they had passed. The phone book lay in shreds on the floor but she didn't need it. Squeezing Saks into the corner behind her, Maeve dialed Emergency Police, cryptically gave her message, and watched the dark crowd of figures surging toward them.

One gang was ahead. The group behind brandished whips and stung the quiet night with loud cracks.

Maeve pushed Saks into the murky sheltered doorway of a coffee shop. They flattened themselves against the dark entrance.

"Don't worry, Saks," Maeve whispered. "The gangs will never see us—they're only after each other, and the cops should be here any minute."

Suddenly, like a rifle shot, a whip cracked.

A single scream followed.

Then, in the middle of the street in plain view, the first group of boys—and girls—skidded to a halt and stood their ground, ready for a return attack with spray-paint cans.

In the misty light of the street lamps, their orange jackets had a satin sheen and across the back was printed *Flames*.

The Whips slid to a stop when they saw the spray-paint cans, and almost in one movement, began a rapid retreat.

But in the general confusion, one of them tangled his own whip around his ankles, hobbling himself, and he fell flat, sprawled full length at the feet of his enemies.

He scrambled up, but his gang had gone, the sound of their running feet already less distinct. The Flames did not give chase. They were satisfied to have a hostage.

The boy cast his eyes on his whip, but one of the Flames kicked it out of reach onto the sidewalk, where it curled around like a dead reptile.

The Flame gang hustled the boy out of sight toward the building next to the coffee shop. Again the street was as quiet as the grave.

Maeve edged out of her corner and peered around the door's recess. The Flames were in a semicircle, facing the one Whip with his back to the wall of the building. The boy's eyes were brimmed with terror and his face was bloodless. The Flames were motionless except one. They were all watching the boy holding a spray-paint can.

104

As Maeve watched, she understood a far greater horror than spray paint itself. The leader of the Flames held a cigarette lighter in his other hand and would light the spray to make a flamethrower.

She screamed, "Stop! Stop!" just as he lit the spray. Startled by her scream, he whirled, the flash of fire shooting high on the building.

"You can't do that," she yelled. "Throw it in the street —you'll burn him!"

When the surprised gang saw Maeve—only a *girl*—they laughed raucously.

The leader said, "Sure—he's barbecue—you, too, if you don't stop screaming—"

Maeve stooped and grabbed the wooden handle of the abandoned whip. She struck him with all her strength just behind the ear. His eyes opened wide, the stream of flame zigzagged drunkenly on the building; the spray can slipped from his fingers as fire sizzled down the wall, singed Maeve's hair, ignited her jacket.

The boy sagged and crumpled on the sidewalk. His astonished comrades stared without moving. Maeve intended to break his fall, but she didn't know her jacket was on fire. Saks jerked Maeve's arms backward, tore the jacket from her and rolled it in a ball to douse the flames. She threw the smoldering fabric into the street.

Maeve knelt by the boy and held her handkerchief to the freely bleeding wound behind his ear.

The gang, now angry, turned on Maeve and Saks. When another one lit a spray-paint can, Saks glared at him, her eyes twin beams of green fire. He was so surprised that he momentarily froze, the flash of fire from the can sending flames writhing down the building like a great orange snake.

Saks couldn't resist it. She shot emerald beams at the flaming snake and suddenly huge glittering green eyes appeared on the wall and showered the gang with flying sparks.

Paralyzed at the sight, their own eyes bulged from their faces. Then, screaming, they ran.

They sprinted down the middle of the street, recklessly bumping each other, glancing fearfully over their shoulders, then speeding pell-mell.

A police car screeched to a stop at the far corner, blocking their exit. Another police car blocked the corner near where Maeve stooped beside the boy. She looked up to see the tallest Flame, babbling, cling to a policeman. "That bag lady . . . that bag lady . . . she . . . she . . ." The boy slid down the policeman and hugged his knees.

A voice from behind Maeve said, "I'll take over now. Are you the vet who put in the emergency call?" A policeman with a first aid kit bent beside the boy as Maeve stood up.

"Yes, I am," she said.

The Flame opened his eyes when the policeman covered him with a woolen wrap. He pointed at Maeve and said in a loud voice, "She hit me! That girl hit me, knocked me out with a metal bar when I didn't do a *thing* to her or that old bag lady. I was just going to catch my bus."

The policeman continued to tuck the woolen wrap around him while the boy spluttered on. "She *did*. She creamed me with a metal bar and knocked me out. I didn't do nothing to her—"

Maeve, exhausted, sat down on the damp curb, and Saks

snuggled close to her. "Couldn't we be going now?" Saks asked. "This rain is cold and it's already daylight."

"I think I'll have to talk to the police first," Maeve answered, watching the boys being ushered into the two police cars. Her eyes burned, her singed hair reeked. She wanted to lie down on the sidewalk and sleep. A soft snore on her shoulder told her that Saks had already folded.

When car doors slammed, Maeve glanced up. A policeman was approaching her, his frown deep and his face stern. She was suddenly worried about the statement the injured boy had made. She started to rise, but the policeman broke into a smile and said, "Don't get up."

He sat down on the curb beside her and placed his notebook on his knee.

"Now, Doctor," he said, "tell me what really happened. The members of the gang said you struck that young man and knocked him unconscious. Is that true?"

Maeve sighed. "Yes, it is," and then with Saks snoring louder and louder on her shoulder, she told him why.

Maeve headed for the shower as soon as she returned to the animal hospital. Saks trailed at her heels though Maeve had asked her to go to the waiting room.

"Maeve, Maeve." A click of heels in the hallway identified Dawn, the temporary receptionist. When Maeve turned, Dawn's eyes opened in shock at Maeve's face, her singed hair, the freckles of soot down the front of her shirt. For a moment she simply stared, then swallowed.

"Good grief! You look terrible." She wrinkled her nose. "And you smell, too." She seemed startled by her own words.

"I mean you smell like smoke or burning things or . . ." She stopped at Maeve's look of impatience.

Maeve blew out a breath of air. Then she said, "I know all that, Dawn. Why are you calling me? And make it fast, will you? I want to get in the shower."

Dawn's hand flew to her bright red lips, smearing scarlet under her nose. "Well, it's just that he's been waiting two hours and I thought you might see him, but . . ."

In surprise, Maeve answered, "Not that bulldog HBC?"

Dawn looked bewildered. "HBC?"

"Hit-by-car, Dawn. I know he needs to be looked at, but I thought one of the other interns would see him while I was at the zoo. But you're right. I don't want those stitches to get infected." She turned back toward the ward.

Dawn clicked a step forward, teetering on her heels. "No, Jim saw the bulldog and what I'm talking about is the bird man."

Maeve stared at her blankly. *"Bird man?"*

"Uh . . ." Dawn frowned, trying to remember the name. "Uh . . . Dr. . . . Dr. . . . Phillips. That's it, Phillips."

Maeve wondered who Dr. Phillips was and what he wanted with her. She was so tired she felt scatterbrained. Then it hit her. The job interview! She had completely forgotten in the events of the night. But she couldn't see him *now*, acrid with smoke and soot. "Dawn, didn't he have some other interviews with the interns? Schedule those while I get cleaned up."

Dawn shook her turquoise ringlets. "He's already seen them. Dr. Magee went in and told him about last night and said you probably wouldn't see him today, but he waited anyway." She twisted one hip in a way that made Maeve think the girl might permanently sprain her back. "You ought to see him, Maeve." Dawn batted her heavy black eyelashes. "He's a real hunk, I mean, a *hunk*. Eyes like blueberries and chocolate hair and kind of mocha skin from the sun and teeth like white frosting!"

"You're making him sound like some kind of cake, Dawn," Maeve said. Amazing the details the temp could remember when she was interested.

Dawn twittered. "Well, he *is* a kind of cake, you'll see. And he's *so* nice. I was talking to him a lot just to . . ." She looked very serious. ". . . just to help pass the time, you know, because he had to wait so long."

I'll bet you did, thought Maeve.

Saks spoke for the first time. "Go see him. I want to see this cake, too."

"I'm going to see him, but not because he looks like a cake, but because I agreed to the interview." She looked at Saks forcefully. "And *you* are *not* coming with me. That's inappropriate for a job interview. *You* are going to the waiting room. We'll have the interview in the lounge."

Saks's lips pushed out in a pout, but she said nothing.

Dawn looked Maeve up and down and then exclaimed, "You're not going to let him see you like *that*, are you?"

"Yes, I am. I don't have to be ice cream to his cake. Now, will you take Saks with you and then ask Dr. Phillips to come to the lounge next door?" She leaned close to Dawn and said, "Dr. Phillips is *not* a bird man, Dawn. He is an ornithologist. *Ornithologist*. Have you got that?"

Dawn looked at her wild-eyed and then, with Saks in tow,

clicked toward the waiting room, muttering, "Ornithologist, ornithologist, ornithologist, ornithol—" until she was out of earshot.

Dr. Phillips was standing with his back to her when Maeve entered the lounge. When he saw her, he held out his hand. Maeve had to admit that every detail the receptionist had described was accurate. She also saw what he had been observing when she came into the room: a large slate-colored African gray parrot, its scarlet tail feathers shimmering brilliantly in the fluorescent light. The bird turned a malicious round eye on Maeve as it perched on the back of a chair.

Ornithologist or not, Maeve thought, the guy is some kind of nut for bringing his parrot to an interview. Is he going to test my knowledge of birds? I'm not a bird specialist.

Politely, after they had introduced themselves, she said, "Beautiful bird."

Dr. Phillips studied the gray parrot for a moment and answered, "Yes, an unusually large one."

"I'm sorry you had to wait but you understand the circumstances, I think, from Dr. Magee."

The conversation went from there to answering Dr. Phillips's interest in the whole previous night, an interest prompted by Maeve's disheveled appearance. Maeve forgot some of her fatigue as her adrenalin flooded again describing the events. Suddenly she was completely taken aback when the parrot fluttered over and landed on her shoulder. She thought Dr. Phillips would immediately reprimand the bird, but all he said was, "Friendly, isn't she?"

Maeve clenched her teeth at the weight on her tired

110

shoulder. "Yes, she is friendly," and she said pointedly, "and *heavy*, too."

He smiled but did not discipline the parrot.

Instead, he said, "You can call me Bill. And you're Maeve, right?"

"Yes," she answered shortly. With the bird's weight forcing her shoulder to sag, her eyes burning still, and her tiredness, and some nut bringing his parrot with him, no matter how much *cake* he was, Maeve decided to end the interview as soon as possible.

"Dr. Phillips, I mean, Bill, I am not an expert on birds. My knowledge is of general animal medicine as I'm sure you know from your own studies. Are you working with exotic birds like this?" She indicated the parrot on her shoulder. The bird rubbed Maeve's nose with the side of its sharp beak. It was all Maeve could do to keep from jumping out of her chair.

Bill didn't say a word to the bird. Maeve thought he was as rude as his crazy, friendly parrot.

At least, I hope it stays friendly, as close to my face as it is, thought Maeve.

Dr. Phillips answered, "Oh, no. We work mostly with native North American birds. We have a small research lab, too, but you would be my assistant as the other two doctors travel a lot as researchers. They only work in the clinic two days a week. That's why we need another doctor."

Maeve was already deciding she wouldn't want to be his assistant, but he warmed to his subject and she didn't interrupt.

"Some of the birds we work with are mallards, green-

111

winged teal, canvasback—lots of ducks. Loons. Lots of loons perish from waste oil from coastal steamers and we try to save those we can. Gannets, great blue herons."

It did sound interesting, Maeve thought. "And what do the researchers do?"

"Different things," he answered. "They teach us. And they solve some greater problems. They have consulted with the insecticide companies, for instance. Robins were dying from eating earthworms who had eaten too much DDT. Whole communities had their robins killed off. They worked out a better way of dealing with insects rather than wholesale spraying. That was a long time ago, but it was a good example."

Maeve looked down at her fingers and said truthfully, "But I hardly know some of the birds you mentioned. I don't think I could qualify."

"Dr. Magee recommended you the most highly of any intern. She said you were diligent and could learn anything you put your head to." He grinned at her. "Listen, I didn't know any more about birds than you do when I started this job. Dr. Hanover and Dr. Welch taught me, and I learned how to deal with damaged eyes of gannets and wood ducks, how to nurture an oil-slick bird. It's fascinating. Birds are such marvelous design. Pelicans, for instance, with their hollow bones filled with air." He was alive with enthusiasm. "They hit the water like a big balloon. They couldn't sink if they tried."

Yes, Maeve thought, *they are fascinating, and little jeweled hummingbirds thrumming with their wings and—*

Shreek! Suddenly a raucous screech split the air. Both

Maeve and Bill were startled. Then Maeve was astonished to hear the parrot in a loud squawk. "Birds are fascinating. Birds are fascinating!"

The voice was extremely loud and the words were clear as a bell.

"Uh . . ." Bill hesitated and then said, "She speaks quite clearly, doesn't she? African grays seem to be the best mimics, but, of course, they have no idea what they are saying."

That crazy bird almost frightened me out of my wits, Maeve thought, *and I don't need you to tell me about bird mimics.* Furiously, she glared at the bird and as if it read her mind, it flew up to the ceiling and then sailed down to plop heavily on Dr. Phillips' shoulder. He flinched and grunted at the landing, then smiled wanly.

If it were my beautiful bird, Maeve thought, *I would teach it some beautiful manners,* and she rubbed her shoulder.

"And the place is in Maine?" Maeve asked.

"Yes, it's in the north woods—a beautiful spot, really, but nothing like New York City. We would have to hike in the last few miles. I could meet you and take you in."

Suddenly the parrot flew from Bill's shoulder and circled around the ceiling screaming, "He's a hunk! He's a hunk! He's a birthday cake! Go with him! He's a birthday cake!"

Maeve glared at Bill furiously but he didn't move, though the skin described by the receptionist as "mocha" flushed a deep cranberry. The bird's voice had a screechy, high-pitched quality which scraped on Maeve's nerves like a fingernail on a blackboard. And the parrot continued. Whishing and swishing and flapping the wings, it circled. "He's a hunk! Go with him. He's a birthday cake!"

Maeve jumped up and shrieked over the bird's racket. "*Yes*, it's interesting! *Yes*, I like the sound of it! *Yes*, I would do it—but I can't stand *you*! I wouldn't work with you if this were the last job on earth!"

She stopped for breath. Bill stared at her openmouthed as she went on. "Common sense ought to tell you not to let your pets run over you, if your training hasn't! That's the rudest bird I've ever heard and it was unprofessional to bring it to this interview!"

Bill stood up but he still seemed to be in shock. The parrot hadn't slowed at all and was still shrieking, "He's a hunk, he's a cake, he's . . ."

Maeve threw her hands over her ears and screamed at the top of her voice, "Tell your bird to *shut up!*"

Bill shook his head violently before he got his words out. "My bird? It's not *my* bird! I thought it was *yours*!" His surprise turned to outrage. "I'd never let a pet act like that! I never saw that raucous parrot before in my life! I was beginning to question your competence no matter *what* Dr. Magee said." He glared back at Maeve, his eyes a darker blue. "It's *your* hospital!"

Maeve turned white, then in a moment, bright red. As suddenly as she had begun, the parrot flapped to the back of a chair and settled. She began to preen her glistening blue-gray feathers as if nothing had happened.

Maeve picked up the intercom, watching the devilish parrot all the while. "Sam? One of the patients, an African gray parrot, has been raising a racket in the lounge. Will you come get it?" She listened for a moment. "I'm going down to the cafeteria to finish this interview." She slapped the intercom speaker back on the wall, and still blushing, motioned an indignant Dr. Phillips to follow.

Her head spun with embarrassment: she was going to have to apologize for herself, for the hospital, probably for the whole New York Society of Veterinarians, for . . .

Clickety-click. The staccato sound of the receptionist's heels announced her.

"Maeve!" Dawn was rushing toward them in the hall as rapidly as her sashaying walk would allow.

"Maeve, your—ah—*friend* went out, but now she's back and she's stretched out on the benches with the animals—*sleeping.*" Dawn flipped her hands in the air as if they were wet. "What shall I do?"

"Put a pillow under her head."

Maeve pivoted quickly and continued toward the cafeteria with a solemn-faced Dr. Phillips. Then she relented and said, "No, on second thought, she needs some breakfast—and so do I."

Rain outside pelted the acrylic walls as they went through the cafeteria line. Other tired interns in their pale green suits were getting coffee or tea and there was a table of white-coated teachers hived in deep discussion on the far side of the room. Bill had only apple juice, Maeve chose oatmeal, strawberries, and toast, and Saks loaded her tray with pancakes and sausage, maple syrup, a bowl of bananas, and a glass of milk. She did not utter a word while Maeve and Bill talked; she was far too busy eating.

Maeve apologized profusely for the parrot's behavior and her own, but Bill finished the episode by laughing about it.

He told her they lost a chef at the research center because a gannet wandered into the cookhouse and ate all the cheese puffs the cook had spent the day making. He said, "He quit on the spot. And he was the best cook we ever had. It's not easy to find a good chef in the north woods."

Maeve smiled, recalling what her grandmother had told her.

"There's a story in my family about that part of the world, southern Canada. The whole settlement was sick and they thought the settlers had caught the disease from the Indians."

Bill sniffed. "More likely, the Indians caught it from the Europeans."

"No, it was not a contagious disease. It was scurvy. They had no citrus or green stuff—no Vitamin C—only meat and cornmeal for months."

Dr. Phillips smiled. "I know that legend. And a pioneer woman, advised by an owl—more probably an Iroquois—made medicine from spruce needles and bark. They all healed like magic because the spruce had Vitamin C. And that was one of your family?"

Maeve showed him the medallion with the broken chain. "That was my many times great-grandmother, way back. This medallion belonged to her. It's so old and thin, I had to have it set in acrylic." Maeve held the scrollwork in her fingers and looked at Bill. "There are some strange bird stories in my family, and some are pretty off-the-wall. They're good tales, anyway."

"I'd like to hear them. If you are free tomorrow—I know you're tired now—could we see the aviary at the zoo and then have lunch?"

Before Maeve could answer, Saks clattered her dishes into a pile and stood up with her empty tray.

"I'll take your dishes back, Saks," Maeve said.

"I'm going to get some scrambled eggs and bacon and French toast," she answered.

Maeve was surprised, but she handed Saks her meal ticket. Bill hid his laughter behind his hand.

"Your friend likes to eat," he said.

"Yes, she does. Now about tomorrow. That will be fine. Shall we meet here about ten?"

They agreed on the time and Saks returned to the table with her plate stacked with food. Bill had arranged to have a volunteer show him around the hospital and he excused himself as Saks dug into her second breakfast.

Maeve said, "He's an okay guy, that Bill Phillips. He can't help being good-looking any more than I can help having red hair." Maeve got a cup of tea and returned to the table. "In a way, that crazy parrot broke the ice for us. Thank heavens Bill has a sense of humor."

Saks had finished her scrambled eggs and bacon and was soaking her French toast in maple syrup.

"You know," Maeve continued, "the staff has not found that parrot. It must have gotten into one of the storerooms or something. It's strange because *expensive* African gray parrots don't just go flying around New York City."

Saks reached for the leftover toast on Maeve's plate and sopped up the rest of the maple syrup until her plate was shiny clean.

"I think I'll like the north woods," Maeve mused, watching the pedestrians outside, the colors of their umbrellas muted by the rain.

Saks suddenly said, "Lots of snow up there in the winter."

"Oh, you've been there. Did you like it?" Maeve asked.

Saks wiped her sticky mouth with her napkin and answered, "It's all right if you're a Great Snowy Owl."

Maeve laughed. "Hey, are you ever serious?"

Saks brushed crumbs from her mangy-looking fur vest and stood up. "I'm going now."

"But it's raining like mad. Wait till it slacks up. Where are you going?" Maeve asked.

"I'm flying to the south of France," answered Saks.

"Oh, Saks," Maeve shook her head and laughed. "At least, take my umbrella. It's in that locker where I put your bag with a black slicker and rain boots." She smiled at the old woman. "If you're back this way again, you can leave it for me." Maeve rose. "I'll get it for you. I'm going to shower anyway."

When Maeve came out of the shower, Saks had already gone. Wrapped in her towel, Maeve looked out. Among the brightly colored umbrellas on the street, she saw her own black one—*and* her black slicker. It was far too long for Saks and was dragging on the wet street. Maeve's rain boots were gone, too. She wondered how Saks, with her small feet, could walk in them. She watched the black speck grow smaller and smaller and then she thought she saw a transparent bird— a huge crystalline bird as clear as rain—rise with something black in its talons. She scrubbed the acrylic to see better but the water drenching the wall was a deluge. She rubbed her eyes.

I am really too tired. I'm seeing things.

What an outrageous character, that Saks. It seemed to

Maeve that she had known her far longer than a few hours. She reached in her locker for her clothes and saw that Saks had left a trade for Maeve's umbrella, slicker, and boots. She had left Maeve her tattered lace kerchief and her scruffy fur vest. Smiling, Maeve folded them together. They looked to be about a thousand years old.